"ASTONISHING . . . LOVELY . . .
A picaresque, sometimes fantastical sojourning; a
pilgrim's progress."

The Washington Post

"Kadohata has a painter's eye, and her narrator's
scroll is filled with scrupulously detailed portraits."

Time

"Luminous . . . A remarkable celebration of
family . . . THE FLOATING WORLD is
exceptional for its quiet humor, its intelligent
revelations and withholdings, and for its careful
depictions of what constitutes love. The carefully
modulated language and manipulation of form
suggests a writer of great maturity; we can
anticipate Ms. Kadohata's next book."

Atlanta Journal & Constitution

"Cynthia Kadohata's marvelous first novel has an
artfully mysterious, dreamlike quality. . . . Kadohata
writes with the coiled intensity of the snake about to
strike."

Newsday

"Evocative . . . The voice that comes through is clear,
melodious, and never rises with emotion or is thrown
off balance. The perceptions have a crisp economy,
and, at moments, something of the ethereal brevity
of a haiku."

Elle

THE FLOATING WORLD

Cynthia Kadohata

BALLANTINE BOOKS · NEW YORK

Copyright © 1989 by Cynthia Kadohata

Portions of this book first appeared in *Grand Street* as "Seven Moons," in *The New Yorker* as "Charlie O," "Jack's Girl," and "Marigolds," and in *The Pennsylvania Review* as "Singing Apples."

Library of Congress Catalog Card Number: 88-40481

ISBN 0-345-36756-1

This edition published by arrangement with Viking Penguin, a division of Penguin Books USA Inc.

Manufactured in the United States of America

First Ballantine Books Edition: April 1991
Third Printing: October 1991

FOR MY MOTHER AND ALL
OF MY FAMILY

Acknowledgments

The author would like to thank Daniel Menaker, her editor at *The New Yorker*, for his insight and kindness; everyone at Viking; and Andre Wylie.

THE
FLOATING
WORLD =

literal translation of
ukiyote.

~ *floating life*
~ *Relate to homeless people / outsiders*

✳✳ My grandmother has always been my tormentor. My mother said she'd been a young woman of spirit; but she was an old woman of fire. In her day it had been considered scandalous for young Japanese women to smoke, but she smoked cigars. Once, when she got especially angry, she took a piece of damp cosmetic cotton and placed it on my ankle so I would hear the sizzle of cotton and think it was skin burning. Later *she* cried. Of the four of us kids, I thought she liked me least. My mother said she didn't dislike me but just expected more of me because I was the oldest.

My grandmother surprised my family by dying one night in a motel in California. Neither of my three brothers liked her any more than I did, and none of us cried at the funeral. My grandmother used to box our ears whenever she pleased, and liked to predict ghastly futures for all of us. We traveled a great deal, and sometimes in the car she talked on and on, until even my mother became annoyed and told her to keep it *down*, just as if she were one of us kids. When she got mad she cursed me. "May you grow hair on your nose!" she would say, and I would run to check a mirror.

Her name was Hisae Fujiitano, a name sort of partway between mine and those of my ancestors. You can trace some of the changes in my family through the changes in our names. In 1875, for the first time, the parents of all my great-grandparents took family names: Yanagita, Osaka (my father's name), Nambu, Takeda, and four Satōs. Before the 1870s, most commoners in Japan were not allowed family names. When the names finally were allowed, sometimes everybody in a village was ordered to take the same one: thus the four Satōs. My mother's mother was born Satō Hisae in a village of Satōs. But though Hisae was her given name, my great-grandparents call her Shimeko, which isn't a real name. "Shimeru" means "to close." They called her Shimeko because she was their eighth child and they hoped that from then on my great-grandmother's womb would be closed.

When Hisae's family came to the United States, her father changed their name to go with their new life. The new name was Fujiitano. Fujii had been the richest man my great-grandfather had ever known, and Itano the happiest. Years later, in Hawaii at the start of World War II, the local school made my grandparents change their children's first names before they could enroll. Satoru, Yukiko, Mariko, Haruko, and Sadamu became Roger, Lily, Laura, Ann, and Roy. Today their original names are just shadows following them. My brothers and I all have American names: Benjamin Todd, Walker Roy, Peter Edward, and me, Olivia Ann.

Before my grandmother died, she told me everything about herself. Sometimes, sitting next to me, she might suddenly grab my hair and pull me over to tell me one more fact about herself: how she had never seen a book until she was twelve, or how she had never cut her long, long hair. She lived with us after her third husband died. But my brothers and I were way ahead of her. Right before she moved in, we gave her a neck chain with a bell attached so we would always hear her approaching and could hide before she reached us. We bought her the bell one Christmas, and she always wore it.

My grandmother liked to tell us about herself during evenings while we all sat talking in front of the motels or houses we stayed at. We were traveling then in what she called ukiyo, the floating world. The floating world was the gas station attendants, restaurants, and jobs we depended on, the motel towns floating in the middle of fields and mountains. In old Japan, ukiyo meant the districts full of brothels, teahouses,

and public baths, but it also referred to change and the plea-
sures and loneliness change brings. For a long time, I never
exactly thought of us as part of any of that, though. *We* were
stable, traveling through an unstable world while my father
looked for jobs.

It seemed as if we were always the only family at the
motels we stayed at, and the proprietors often gave my
brothers and me candy, matches, or gum. We saved most
of what we got, and sometimes as my grandmother told
stories we would make trades with each other: matches
for gum, candy for matches. I had a special piece of
chocolate that I'd had for three years and would never
trade. Sometimes I licked it, for luck.

My grandmother owned a valise in which she carried all
her possessions, but the stories she told were also possessions. The stories were fantastic, yet I believed them. She
said that when she was young fireflies had invaded her
town, so the whole town was lighted even during the night-
time. She said she had been told that the summer she was
born, strange clouds passed through the sky. Every night for
seven nights, a different cloud. The clouds all had a strange
glow, as if someone had taken the moon and stretched it into
a cloud shape. Those seven moon-clouds, she said, had been
a lucky omen. As she spoke, she always gestured a great
deal, so the background to her stories would be the soft tinkling of the bell we had bought her.

She did most of the talking, but once in a while one of my
parents spoke up to amplify or to make their own, new con-
tributions. Other times, my parents might gently indicate that
she should stop talking because it was our bedtime, or because they did not approve of the subject. No matter—if she
wanted to tell me something she would seek me out later.
She would run after me, shouting her facts: I had a white
dog! I broke my leg three times! My first husband and I had
sex in a public bathroom!

Sometimes my father did seasonal farming work and my
mother helped out, but mostly he found work as a body-and-
fender man or a carpenter. We sometimes traveled in the

Pacific states with one or two other young Japanese families, heading for jobs the fathers had heard of. We moved often for three reasons. One was bad luck—the businesses my father worked for happened to go under, or the next job we headed to evaporated while we were in transit. Also, it could be hard even into the fifties and sixties for Japanese to get good jobs. Nothing was ever quite the position my father felt he deserved. The third reason was that my parents were dissatisfied with their marriage, and, somehow, moving seemed to give vent to that dissatisfaction. It was always hard to leave our homes, but once we started traveling, a part of me loved that life. All the packing and moving was especially hard on my parents, but I think even they enjoyed some of the long drives—at least, they did when my grandmother was quiet. I remember how fine it was to drive through the passage of light from morning to noon to night.

What I learned, traveling in Oregon, Wyoming, California, and Washington, was that my first grandfather had drowned off the coast of Honolulu. My third, I knew, had died of old age. My grandmother said she was still married when she met her third husband. She had been trying to fix him up with a woman from Japan, but he decided he wanted to marry her instead. He begged her to leave her second husband, and she couldn't resist his begging.

"You couldn't resist because you loved him so much?" I said. "You couldn't resist because he was so handsome?"

"I couldn't resist because his begging was like buzzing in my ears," she said. "I had to make it stop." She hit one of her ears as if to stop some buzzing.

Actually, it was my mother, one evening when we were in northern California, who told me her father had drowned. We were staying at a place someone had lent us while my father had a temporary job helping a friend build a farmhouse. When he finished with this job, we would be on our way to Arkansas, where my father was going to buy into a garage another friend of his owned. "It'll be the first time I've ever owned anything big," he said. "A car don't count."

I was sitting on the porch with my mother and brothers.

My father had already gone inside to take a shower and go to bed, and my grandmother was napping.

"Olivia, go get Obāsan," said my mother. "It's pretty out here. She should see." Two Japanese words for "grandmother" are "obāsan" and "obāchan." You call your grandmother Obāsan if you're not close to her, Obāchan if you are. I think my mother would have liked for us to call our grandmother Obāchan, but we never did. We called her Obāsan. My father wanted us to call her Grandma—more American.

Ben and Walker looked at me. We took daily turns dealing with Obāsan. Ben was eight, four years younger than I; Walker was seven; and Peter, two. Ben was the opposite of Walker, outgoing and talkative where Walker was quiet and brooding. I was sort of outgoing and quiet both, depending.

"I think it's Ben's turn," I said.

His jaw dropped in outrage. "No. Remember, I gave you gum and you said you would take my turn."

He was right—I had the gum in my mouth. I tried to swallow it and almost choked. So I went inside. The house was one room. The light was very low, barely good enough to read in, and the room was smoky from my grandmother's cigars.

"What do you want?" said Obasan.

She took an ominous step toward me with her cigar and I got scared and ran. When I got outside and saw my mother, I remembered she'd wanted me to get my grandmother. So I turned around and shouted as loudly as I could, "Mom wants you!" When I saw her at the door I turned to my mother, who was standing right next to me. "She's coming," I said.

"Goodness," said my mother.

My grandmother sat outside with us, and after a while, when I'd decided she was in a good mood, I asked her whether she'd cried for weeks after her first and third husbands died.

"Does a slave cry when the master dies?"

"It depends," I said. "Did you love any of your husbands?"

She paused, and I could see that she had loved one of them. But she didn't say so. She said, "I loved all of them in a way, and none of them in a way."

"So why get married?"

"Because they asked." I knew that Japanese women were nothing without husbands, and she probably had not wanted to be nothing.

"I remember the day my father drowned," said my mother. We always got extra quiet when my mother spoke. This was the first I'd heard of any drowning. My mother rarely initiated small talk, and usually when she spoke she had something she especially wanted to say. She had an elegant, lush face, and always had about her a slight air of being disoriented, as if she could not quite remember how she came to be wherever she was. I think sometimes people interpreted that disoriented air as aloofness. "When I found out what had happened to him, I went outside and wandered around for hours, and I found a wooden rose in a field. It had the look, texture, and strength of a piece of carved wood, but it was a real flower. It was alive. I've never found a reference to a wooden rose in books on flowers, but I'm sure it existed. I remember thinking it was impossible, just like my father's death was impossible. For a few hours, I was in another realm, and impossible things happened."

The house my father had been working on sat way in the distance. The family would be moving there the following week. Fireflies hovered around the house, but they weren't the fireflies of my grandmother's childhood invasion. They blinked like Christmas lights. They made the house seem enchanted. I thought how lucky some children would be to live in a place like that.

My grandmother pushed my head down suddenly so that the side of my face was pressed against the concrete porch. "Be careful you never marry anyone who's going to die young," she said.

I tried to say okay, but my mouth was being squished by her hand, so I said, "Uh-keh."

She let me go and wiped her nose with the back of her hand. I sat up and saw my big wad of gum sitting on the porch. I dusted it off, plunked it into my mouth, and blew a big bubble to show my grandmother she didn't bother me. In truth, I was shaking inside. But anyway I thought I had found out something I'd wanted to know—it was her first husband she'd loved. I liked finding out things about her. I just wished it weren't such hard work.

In the mornings, Obāsan always took my brothers and me for walks, but in the evenings she liked to go for drives. I always went with her, because my mother made me, "just in case something happens," she said. My brothers were too young to go, and my mother and father were always too tired. When I wanted to go somewhere at night, my parents asked my grandmother to accompany me—just in case. So my life intertwined with my grandmother's.

That night, we went for one of her drives in my father's gray, whale-shaped car. She was so tiny she had to sit on two pillows, way forward on the seat. One good thing about her drives was that I was always seeing something surprising—a pet camel in someone's backyard, or a set of elderly men triplets, dressed the same way down to their canes. I liked downtowns the best, the way the neon and shadows cut into each other when the streets were empty. Whenever we waited at a stop sign or traffic light, my grandmother clicked her arthritic knee—it sounded as if she were clicking her toenails against something. I had no idea what Obāsan saw that she liked, or what she got out of those drives. Sometimes she tricked me into not hating her. She gave me change to buy candy, or she let me drive for a couple of minutes. But pretty soon she would be the same again—cruel, name-calling, quick-tempered.

After we'd driven in circles for a while, she said she needed to use the bathroom, and she left me to sit in the car while she walked off into the darkness. We were not far from where we were staying, and I spotted a man who owned a nearby farm walking toward the car. I hadn't met him, but my mother had pointed him out before. He was easy to recognize, tall, with only one eyebrow, big and black like an extra eye. He was drinking from a paper cup, and I went out to call him—maybe he would let me have a sip of whatever he was drinking.

I liked to talk to strangers. My parents were proud of the way I talked. "If you couldn't see her, you wouldn't even know she was Japanese," they would say. When I spoke with outsiders I was showing off, but they never understood this. I was trying to impress them, to make them like me. But at the same time I was always taunting them. See, I can talk like you, I was trying to say, it's not so hard. My grandmother didn't like that I wanted to impress them, but she liked the taunting part. "Smile at them," she would say. "Hakujin don't know when a smile is an insult." Hakujin were white people. She always said her experience showed that if you hated white people, they would just hate you back, and nothing would change in the world; and if you didn't hate them after the way they treated you, you would end up hating yourself, and nothing would change that way, either. So it was no good to hate them, and it was no good not to hate them. So nothing changed.

"Hi," I said to the man who owned the farm. He didn't answer, so I went on. "What are you drinking?"

"Coffee."

"Oh." He sat down on the hood of the car and crossed his legs. I climbed on the hood and sat next to him.

He swept his hand toward the landscape. "Where do you locate your expertise in this world?" he said.

"Excuse me?" There was something strange about him, besides the way he talked, but I couldn't put my finger on what it was. I peeked into his cup to see how much was left: not much.

He told me he used to teach at a university, and his question simply meant "Who are you?" I didn't think they would let someone who talked the way he did teach at a university, but of course that was before I ever went to college.

"How come you stopped teaching?"

"Because I killed someone."

I thought he meant in a car accident or something, and I started to say "I'm sorry," but I stopped myself. Another car drove by, illuminating his face, and I saw what was so strange about him. He wasn't who I thought he was, not the farmer at all. I saw angles on his face where I thought there had been slopes, and he had a flesh-colored bandage, partly hidden by hair, over one of his eyebrows.

"You have two eyebrows!" I said. "You're no farmer."

He paused, I see now because he didn't know what I was talking about. But I thought I had stunned him with truth.

I stood straight; then he did, too. The way he moved, so relaxed, it seemed he moved slowly, but really the movement had been swift. I climbed casually back on the car, and he sat down again, too.

"I have to get going in a sec," I said, faking a yawn. I thought things over. I wasn't scared exactly. I figured maybe Obāsan had somehow arranged all this to scare me. Then I remembered what my mother had said about the wooden rose, and I felt as if maybe I was in that other realm now, and I could get hurt. I stood up, and the man did, too. He really was big—and he seemed to have grown in the last few minutes. Whereas before I thought I'd reached his chest, I now reached his waist. All of a sudden he tilted his head, listening. Then I heard it, too, the tinkling of a bell, getting closer behind us.

We both turned to look, and my grandmother walked up and stopped a few feet from the other side of the car. Maybe my demeanor told her something, because she seemed to sense my fear. She smiled her widest smile at the man. She didn't smile often, and if you saw her you would know why. Her smile made her look as if she had a stomachache. Though we were staring straight at her, she announced shrilly, "I'm back." She and the man looked at each other for a long minute, and then she leaned over, still smiling, and picked

up a stick from the ground. She came forward, waving the
stick and repeating shrilly, "I'm back. I'm back. I'm back."

The man left then. He walked the way he'd stood up before, an illusory slow motion, but really he moved very
quickly. I watched him get smaller and smaller as he walked
away.

"That man was going to kill me."

"I should have let him."

We got in the car. I thought the only reason she'd scared
the man away was so my mother wouldn't get angry with her
if something happened to me. I was sick of her meanness,
her insults, her hatred. I decided not to speak to her again
for as long as I could, maybe a week, or even two. And if
she wanted to go for a ride I would refuse to go.

She drove as usual, with lots of stops and jerks. She didn't
speak, either. Once, maybe when she thought I wasn't looking, she glanced at her hand, and I saw several deep inden-
tations and a thin cut on her palm. She gave me a sharp look.
"Mind your own business, nosy girl," she said. It took me
a moment to realize what had happened—she'd been squeezing the stick so hard it cut into her hand. I bet she would
have killed that man had he tried to hurt me.

Later, in bed, I was the last one up, as usual. Ben and
Walker, covered by sheets, were white humps on the floor,
and Peter slept in a crib we'd borrowed. My parents, lying
unusually close together, looked like one larger person. My
grandmother was on her side, her sheet hanging off the bed,
one of her breasts hanging out of her nightgown. Her breast
was smooth and white, in contrast to her ravaged, red face.
I pressed my fingers over my nipples and ran my fingers up
my chest and neck and face—the same smooth skin all over.
It was hard for me to picture how a baby girl whose birth had
been marked by seven moons floating across the summer sky
had come to be in this house, and had come to be the person
she was—unhappy, cruel, the nemesis of her grandchildren.
I tried to imagine this happening. But there were windows

all over, and the wind passed over me, back and forth, back and forth, until it seemed, at the time, that I had more important things to imagine.

※※ *2*

※※ Sometimes as I lay awake in bed I made up fantasies. I imagined something awful, like my parents getting killed, or that I was a grownup and a man I loved died. At the end of my fantasy my stomach would hurt or I would cry. The point of these fantasies was to make my stomach hurt. When I was little my parents had to take me to the doctor because I got ulcers.

Other times, I thought about things that had already happened, moments or days or years ago. A gargoyle on the front door of this house reminded me of a house with a gargoyle I lived in a couple of years earlier.

My parents were broke and having marriage problems, and two of my brothers and I went to stay with a foster parent in Nebraska. His name was Isamu, and my father knew him from a farm they'd both worked on in California. He was a little crazy, in my opinion, but my father trusted him.

Peter, who'd just been born, went to stay with one of my mother's sisters. Ben, Walker, and I couldn't stay with any of my mother's four brothers and sisters, because they already had twenty-seven children among them. And my parents didn't want us to stay with Obāsan, supposedly because her third husband had just died. I think the real reason was that my grandmother, seventy-three, was consumed with an affair, and my parents thought this might be a bad influence

12

on us. I was all for her having an affair, because if she did she might get married again. If she didn't get married, I feared she would come to live with us eventually. That's what happened—her boyfriend passed away later that year.

Ben, Walker, and I were well behaved in our way, and Isamu hardly ever lost his temper. The only time he got truly mad was at the end of our first week, when he decided we should no longer take baths together.

My brothers and I used to take bubble baths with Tide detergent. We could make bubble forts three feet high. The night we got in trouble, Ben had just climbed into the water— Walker and I were already in the tub—when I noticed that some veins or something on Ben's bottom seemed to spell the word "hello."

"Holy smokes, it's a miracle," I said. "Lean over."

Walker and I were marveling over him when Isamu came in and got really quite alarmed. He hauled us out of the tub and chased us naked from the bathroom. "What are you up to? Are you mad?" he said.

"It's a miracle!" Ben cried as we slipped through the halls. We didn't get to rinse off all night. Later I passed the boys' room and saw Ben, his pants pulled down, trying to view himself in a hand-held mirror. He kept turning slightly to get a better view, but it was a hopeless task. Since I was the oldest, I was the only one who got punished. I had to write "I will be clean and decent" five thousand times. It took me more than a week, and toward the end I used Band-Aids to keep my fingers from blistering.

Isamu's house was eccentric but homey. I liked the kitchen tapestry with the state motto, "Equality Before the Law," but didn't like the stuffed squirrel beneath it. Besides his gargoyle, he owned a couple of other items with faces. A flower vase was shaped like a bunch of broccoli, with eyes near the handles, and two purple glass turtles grinned wildly from a living room bureau.

Isamu had a daughter he was besotted with. Once, she was supposed to come visit by train. We drove thirty miles to the station, but the train was ten hours late. My brothers took naps, but I stayed up, thinking and daydreaming. I dreamed my parents were never coming back. My stomach started to hurt so much I had to stop thinking. Isamu talked about his daughter, what a princess she was, how generous and smart. The wind outside the car knocked over the surrounding weeds, first one way, then the other. The train came, and his daughter wasn't on it. When we got home and called, she explained she'd decided to come another time and had completely forgotten to phone.

We all went outside to sit in back. Isamu turned to us, his eyes ugly and cruel. We froze. He said his daughter was a slut. I didn't know what that meant, but I knew it was awful. Walker's feet had been making scraping sounds in some dry leaves, but the sound stopped abruptly. My brothers and I held hands. I wondered what my parents were doing at that moment, and then I started to worry about Peter, as well. Sometimes my mother let me give him his bath. He had extremely sensitive ears, and if you got even a little water in them he would be in pain for hours. I worried all night, even in bed, that my aunt might not be washing his ears carefully enough.

Obāsan was mumbling in her sleep, but in Japanese, a curse I couldn't quite understand. I figured she must have been dreaming about me.

Neither my parents nor Ben and Walker like to talk much about those days, and one of the few concrete reminders I have of my time in Nebraska is a photograph of my brothers that Isamu took when we first moved in. In the picture they're standing on a crate you can't see, their black tops barely lifted above the surrounding mass of yellow. I'm in the picture, too; if you look closely you can see my hand reaching up between two wheat stalks. Ben used to tease that it was his favorite picture of me.

Once we got used to the place, I started to like my days at Isamu's. They were a brief peaceful pause before Obāsan moved in with my family.

Isamu didn't have many friends. There were no other Japanese in town, and I guess he didn't feel he had much in common with most of the people around. To keep himself busy, he kept a constantly long list of chores for himself. Once, he spent all afternoon choosing an address book. He liked my penmanship and wanted me to write in the names. First he had to decide whom to write down. "Let's see . . . my daughter, my nephew, and my nephew's daughter," he said. "She has her own phone. I think they spoil her."

"What about your gin rummy friends?" He played once a week.

"I don't call them that much. I never write them."

"Didn't you say you had a cousin in Omaha?"

"Oh, right, my cousin. Now how many is that?"

"Four."

He thought awhile. "Okay, write down my gin rummy friends." So he had seven people in his phone book.

The next day his chore was planting a tree. There were about forty trees in the backyard, planted individually on succeeding anniversaries of the day he married his late wife. He still kept this up, though Meg had been gone for eleven years. "Habit," he said. "Anyway, I need the exercise." I watched him dragging the sapling. Stopping, sweating, stopping, sweating. I feared he might faint.

Several months later, our parents came for us on a freezing winter afternoon. They looked slightly different, in that indefinable way people you haven't seen for a while look slightly different. After a few minutes I started to feel shy with them. When we'd first spotted their car coming, we'd been in the front yard, building in the snow with Isamu. Ben saw the car first, and went tearing down the road, screaming and yelling. Then we stopped making noise so we could concentrate better on running our fastest. We were almost to the car when I stopped suddenly. My brothers passed me. I turned around. Isamu looked forlorn, standing alone in all that snow. "Don't leave!" he said. No one else seemed to hear him, or maybe I just imagined it. Then my mother was twirling me through the air, and I thought I would swoon.

After supper my family drove off. We were going to California to pick up Peter. I liked to stick my head out the window, and my mother always gave me permission to open the window for five minutes, no matter how cold it was. I felt the frigid air hit my face. It was dark out. When the plains were white that way, I always had difficulty making out where the earth ended; it was as if the ground simply curled upward. When it was still dark out each morning on the way to our school bus, I used to look at the lighted farmhouses and imagine how cities must be, with lighted houses piled on lighted houses. That's the way I imagined apartments, farmhouse on farmhouse into the sky. In the night I could picture it without even closing my eyes.

I looked at the farmhouses on the ceiling of the house we were staying at. My grandmother's snoring filled the room. She sounded like an elephant with a breathing problem, but we were used to it.

※※ **3**

※※ Sometimes Obāsan slept for hours and hours, until we thought she was sick, while other times she required no sleep at all. Though she and I had returned late the night before, she woke my brothers and me at six, as usual, for our morning hike. We always had to go with her, unless we weren't feeling well. But I didn't mind. Some days, the people we met on those mornings would be the only people I talked to besides my family and whatever family we were traveling with. Those walks were some of my favorite times growing up.

It was still dark gray out. She wanted to take a long walk. My father's job wouldn't be finished until evening, and we had nothing to do all day. We put Peter into a stroller and headed off through a sloping field and some orchards. Peter was used to bumping along. He could sleep through anything. A fine mist broke up our view, as if each drop of mist were a dot of paint. The mist sprayed coolly on our cheeks as we walked through the field, and the long misted grass brushed our ankles. I could feel the blood flowing to my face as I tried to keep up with Obāsan, who always walked briskly.

We saw some kids outside a farm. They'd probably be going to school later. "What's today?" said Walker.

"Wednesday."

"Wednesday." He didn't say anything else. Walker hardly

17

ever talked, except to repeat something just said. Sometimes we called him Echo.

Obāsan had a cigar and stopped to blow smoke rings into the air. The sky, white-gray, showed through the rings.

"Will you smoke when you get older?" Ben asked me.

"I'll never smoke. I want to be the opposite of Obāsan. Anything she does, I never will."

"She eats," said Ben. "And you have to eat." He crossed his eyes at me.

I chased him through the grass, but he stopped abruptly and knelt, and I fell over him. I rolled, just for fun, through the damp field. When I got dizzily to my feet, my grandmother and brothers were watching me. With them stood an old man. That is, his face didn't appear old, but he had wispy white hair that stood on end, seeming to move and fly of its own accord, like something alive. He'd appeared out of nowhere—all around us were fields. I sort of salivated inside whenever I met someone new. I was nosy, and I thought new people might tell me interesting things.

Obāsan didn't speak. There was something imperial about the way she held herself, the way she ignored the man. She appeared to be looking through him, at the sky and the fields. I could see she wasn't going to speak, so I told the man I hoped we weren't trespassing.

He chewed on something and glanced over the beautiful misted fields. The fields were full of varied greens. They were his fields, I felt sure. "Maybe you're trespassing," he said. I felt a brief fear, probably just left over from the night before.

"Sorry."

He chewed some more. The wind blew at his hair. I thought the wispy strands might fly away. "But maybe you're not," he said.

Obāsan continued to gaze through him. "We'll go now," I said. We turned and began to leave. I noticed Obāsan's cigar was gone. I noticed something burning a hole in her pocket. Obāsan, so brave last night, was scared of this man. She was scared of what he might think of her cigar.

"Hey," the man called, and we turned around. "I'll sell you some apples cheap."

Everyone looked at me expectantly. "What kind of apples?"

"What kind do you want?"

"Well, are they good?"

"The best."

The hole in my grandmother's pocket had stopped smoking.

We went with the man to buy some apples. Men had come out to work some of the fields. The men touched their hats when they said "Good morning" to me and my grandmother, and I felt very grown up.

"Where are you all from?" said the man.

"Here and there." My grandmother had told me once never to tell people where I came from or what my name was.

He nodded at her. "She speak English?"

I considered this question. Maybe she didn't want me to tell. "I'm not sure," I said, stupidly.

Behind a barn sat several bushels, a couple of them filled with large golden delicious apples, sunbursts of pale rose and green on the rich yellow skins. We pooled our money— Obāsan had most—and bought two dozen apples. My grandmother owned a magic purse that never emptied, though she didn't work and had never made much money. She always had a couple of dollars.

"You know how to pick good apples?" said the man.

"Color?" said Ben.

"Nope."

"Smell?"

"Nope." He paused before saying with mock impatience, "Do you want me to tell you or not?" He paused again, throwing an apple into the air. Finally he said triumphantly: "Sound." He squeezed and rubbed the apple between his large hands until it squeaked. "Good one," he said. "It sings. Never buy an apple unless it sings." He added hurriedly, "Of course the ones you just bought are all good." He rubbed and rubbed, making three distinct notes, enough for "Mary Had a Little Lamb" and another song I didn't recognize, and he moved his head in time with the music, his hair following the movement of his head. We also tried to play the apples, but ours sounded like tiny sick cows.

We headed back without the man. I felt very happy, almost elated, for no real reason, just for the way the morning had started. The workers in the fields stopped again to touch their hats.

"Hey!"

We turned around, saw the man standing in the distant mist.

"Someday you teach your kids that apple trick!" he called. He tapped at the space above his head as if he wore a hat, and then walked off with his dancing hair, and with his singing apple still in hand.

He'd given us no bags, so we had trouble carrying the apples. Obāsan walked way ahead with Peter. We kept dropping the apples, but soon we were having so much fun chasing after the falling fruit that we began to drop it deliberately. As I chased a stray apple, I saw Obāsan stop walking, and I thought she wanted to scold us. But she was staring out over the fields, the way you might stare at someone who is leaving you. She had worked on a celery farm a few seasons, and I wondered whether she was remembering that. Today when I think back on how she looked, I believe she knew then she would die soon. I bit into an apple, and she turned to glare at me. My brothers had run way ahead with the stroller. "Give me that apple." She walked toward me. "Don't eat that."

"How come?"

"It's dirty."

Every time she took a step toward me I took a step back. Sometimes I ran from her, but I never ran hard. I didn't want her to catch and hit me, but I didn't want to lose her, either. It was our responsibility to keep an eye on each other. I continued eating my apple but rolled up the rest of the fruit in my skirt and hurried home, making sure never to lose sight of Obāsan. By the time we got to the house, her face was all evil and anger. I felt scared now, so I ran inside, chained the door, and sat on the bed to finish the apple. I jumped when the door jerked partway open, stopped by the chain. One of Obāsan's eyes peered in. If I squinted, she looked like a Cyclops. I chomped into a new apple, still staring at her. She reached her hand in, jiggling the chain while my heart pounded, but she couldn't open the door. She cajoled, she bribed, she threw kisses. She jangled her purse, suddenly full of coins. "Livvie, my sweet, I have to use the bathroom," she said. But I knew she was lying. I could have closed the door or hidden from sight, and my body jerked with the impulse to get up. Instead I bit into my third apple and felt mesmerized by my grandmother's face.

"I can't open it," I said. "You'll hit me."

She stood there, her arthritic knee clicking. Finally she left, and I didn't hear any clicking or tinkling or muttering. I sneaked to the door and slowly opened it. She was sitting on a little bench on the porch. She had a peaceable look on her face. I went to put the remaining apples next to her and sat on a stair. The mist had risen, covering the sky with gray lace. Something pounded across my ear, knocking me over. "Why did you give that man my money?" Obāsan said.

When my father finished work that evening, we started driving immediately. We were going to visit with relatives in Los Angeles, then head to Arkansas. The Shibatas, a family we'd met that week, were traveling with us to L.A. We stopped for the night at a small motel. That was a long time ago—the motel cost two dollars a night. It had a lighted pink vacancy sign, and another sign reading Cal-Inn. The view was lovely: almond groves made jagged black lines on the horizon, and I thought I smelled almonds in the air. After supper, everyone sat on the curb outside the motel. There were only two cars besides ours and the Shibatas' in the parking lot. My brothers and I and the Shibata children played strings, cards, and jan ken po—the Japanese version of paper-scissors-rock. Then we sat briefly bored, scraping and rapping our bare feet restlessly on the parking lot concrete.

Susie Shibata and I got up to sing for everyone. We did a little dance. I sang more on key, yet her voice held more sweetness, so I sat back and listened. I was singing softly along when Obāsan pushed me from my place at the curb—she'd been sitting behind me, I suppose. Ordinarily I wouldn't have felt indignant, because it had always been a rule that we either must offer our elders our seats or expect to be forcibly removed. But Obāsan had pushed me especially hard this time. And she'd been mean to me while we were cooped up in the car all day. Several times she'd boxed the side of my head and told me to quiet down.

"You made me scrape my knee," I said. I held up my knee, my foot dangling in the air. "See the blood? You're in my seat, and please move now."

"What did you say?" she said. She rubbed her fingers together. I could just hear the dry skin scraping.

She reached out and grabbed my wrist, but I tried to pull it away and run. She held fast, though. I wouldn't have thought she was so strong, but I couldn't get away. We called her Pincher Obāsan behind her back. One of her methods of punishment was to smile as if she loved you with her full heart, all the while squeezing you inside the wrist. You were supposed to smile back as best you could. We had a funny picture of Ben getting pinched. With that smile, he looked like a lunatic. Now I opened my lips, pressed my teeth hard together, and tried to keep my eyes opened wide. Obāsan smiled easily back at me as she pinched. The lighting made her gums look brown, and I knew her top teeth were dentures. I was determined to outsmile her. Once, when she'd got mad at Ben and

pinched him for something like fifteen minutes, he out-
smiled her, and finally she broke down, patted his head,
and gave him a nickel. I would make her give me a nickel,
too. But she didn't stop, and after a while I felt my pulse
between her fingers. I thought a vein would burst, or my
skin might fall off in her hands.

"You've got the record!" encouraged Ben. Meaning it had
been more than fifteen minutes.

Obāsan seemed to pinch more tightly. "All right!" I said.
She let go, and I went off to sit by myself. My mother came
over and ran her hand across my head. When I felt I could
talk without crying, I said, "Mom, I was just sitting there.
She pushed me. You saw."

"She's old," said my mother. "But I'll tell her not to be
so hard on you. Okay?"

"She's evil," I said. "When she smiles I see she's a
devil." I sucked on my wrist.

My mother laughed. "Oh, you never even knew her during her pinching prime. I could tell you stories."

"Obāsan pinching stories!" I said. "That's the last thing
I want to hear."

My father rose to go in, as did Mr. Shibata. "Seven
o'clock?" said my dad. Mr. Shibata nodded. Seven was when
we would start out the next day. Before he went in, my father
knelt beside me and my mother. "How'd you like to sit in
front with us tomorrow?"

"Okay."

"You can have the window if you want or the middle if
you want," said my mother.

"Thank you," I said. But I wasn't appeased.

My father went in. My mother followed with Peter, and I
followed her. I didn't want to sit outside with Obāsan.

My mother sat on the bed and leafed through a book
about presidents' wives. She admired presidents' wives
and liked to know what they ate and wore, liked to know
the odd fact that made them human. For instance, she
liked knowing that Andrew Jackson's wife married him
mistakenly, thinking she'd obtained a divorce from her first

husband, or knowing that Mrs. Polk, who was very religious, prohibited liquor and dancing in the White House—"No wonder the Polks had no children," she would say. She'd probably inherited her interest in first ladies from Obāsan, who used to revere the Japanese emperor and his wife. "The emperor was a moron," Obāsan once said, "but he was still the emperor."

My grandmother came inside; I went out.

It was always a relief when she went in for the evening, but it felt especially wonderful that night. My brothers and I played tag back of the motel, and later we peeked into the rooms of strangers, but saw nothing. When we'd finished playing, only Mrs. Shibata and Susie still sat on the curb.

Though Obāsan always went inside early, she usually came to the door when a car approached the motel office. "Get in. What will people think, with Japanese hanging around like hoodlums at night?" We would all go in, watch until the car had left, then wander out, continuing this wandering in and out until time for bed. But tonight a car drove up and I waited expectantly for Obāsan's voice. When it didn't come I figured she'd gone to sleep, and I turned around, idly, to glance through the open door. I was really quite shocked to see my grandmother, looking cadaverous in the neon, standing in the doorway silently watching the car. She came out and sat with us briefly, an event unprecedented at that hour. She talked of her life. "My memories are a string of pearls and rocks," she said. I thought that was a line she'd memorized to say to us, but then she stretched her bony hands through the air, so for a moment I seemed to see the glitter of the string extended over the concrete lot. But the next moment she turned to me in one of her furies. "*I* don't know," she cried. But I didn't know what she was talking about. It was like the night Isamu got upset because his daughter had failed him. With all the older people I knew, even my parents, I occasionally saw that fierce expression as they exclaimed over something that had happened years ago, losses in a time and place as far removed from my twelve-year-old mind as the dates in a schoolbook.

Later I lay on the floor under the sheets. My wrist still hurt. I couldn't sleep. I watched as my grandmother walked to the bathroom. Obāsan was in there for a long time, and after a while I started to hear noises like coughing. I got up and knocked on the bathroom door, but Obāsan didn't answer.

The door was unlocked, though. Obāsan lay in her housedress on a towel she must have placed on the floor. Though I know now it was just my imagination, at the time I thought she seemed to have been expecting me. She was already not of this world, and she spoke with a fury unnatural even for her. "You! Get your mother," she said. It was a hiss, a rasp, and a cracked whisper all at once. I felt cold, as if there were ghosts in the room. But it was my own body, making me cold in the warm night. I reached back to close the door and turned to watch her again.

"Get your mother," Obāsan said. Still with fury but, now, something else, too. The hint of a "please" in her voice.

I saw in the mirror that I was crying and shaking. I had hated my grandmother for so long.

"Get your mother." This time Obāsan sounded desperate, pleading.

She said it two more times, once with draining hope and the last time peacefully. "Get your mother," she said, with calm, peaceful resignation. She closed her eyes and I left. I got under the sheets again. Dim light shone through the sheet over my head, a glow like very early morning. Sometimes, when I couldn't quite place what I was feeling, I would search through my body, from my toes up to my calves, between my legs, and on up to my head. Now my stomach hurt. I thought I heard noise from the bathroom. Obāsan was ready to die, I thought. And then I felt very sleepy.

When I next woke, Walker had just found Obāsan dead on

the bathroom floor. He clung to me as we stood at the door.
My mother stood over her mother, horrified. My father was
grim.

"She made me kill her!" I said.

"She made me kill her!" Walker echoed.

My parents just thought I was crazy with grief.

We sent Obāsan's body to Wilcox, California, which
was where her third husband was buried, and drove there
for the funeral. As I watched the casket buried, I felt surrounded by a cool, choking swirl of air that made me
cough up phlegm and made my eyes smart and water, and
I knew that Obāsan was there. But the coldness went away,
and it never returned. I looked toward the sky, to see
whether my grandmother's ghost might be heading heaven-
ward. "No, she must have gone down there," I said,
pointing with my thumb toward the ground. I automati-
cally braced myself for the ear boxing I always got when
I said something I knew I shouldn't say; but there would
be no more of that. I placed a bouquet of red plastic flowers on the gravestone.

Peter pointed at the flowers. "Obāsan?" he said—as if the
whole of her life had been distilled into the flash of color in
the gray cemetery.

We headed for Los Angeles to visit relatives. On the
drive down we had some of Obāsan's riches—enameled
boxes, painted fans, and old journals filled with graceful
Japanese writing. We had her purse, empty now, and a
picture of her as a striking woman in her twenties. As we
drove, I played the last time I'd talked to her over and over
in my mind, changing the end so that in my fantasies I
went to get my parents for help. But when I emerged from
my fantasy and thought about how evil I had been, I got
a feeling I get sometimes even today, that there are things
I am scared to know. My mother had cut off her mother's
long braid and given one strand each to Ben, Walker, and
me. The strands were black at one end and white at the
other. I tied a string around mine and folded it into one
of the enameled boxes. All the windows in the car were

open. It was early evening, and we were halfway between Wilcox and Los Angeles. I stuck my head out the window. I was free. But I didn't feel free.

✳✳ My grandmother used to talk a lot about the days after she inherited her parents' boardinghouse. When she was gone my brothers begged me to tell them the stories again.

I knew only one of Obāsan's husbands—the last, whom I met a couple of times. Obāsan's father had worked as a fisherman when he came to the States, but so many fights broke out between the white and the Japanese fishermen that he decided to find more peaceful work. He'd saved some money, so he and a brother bought a boardinghouse in San Francisco. That's where my grandmother met her first husband.

Years later, my mother, her older sisters, and a cousin used to help around the house. My mother cut the boarders' hair and cooked breakfast, her sisters cooked supper and lunch, and the cousin kept the kitchen and bathrooms clean. When the house got old and began to fall apart, they used to huddle together in their bedroom and cry. The ceiling had fallen down in the hallway, and because the house was built on soft land, its weight had shifted, and certain doors would no longer close. Eventually, my grandparents sold the house and moved to Hawaii. (That's where my mother, formerly Mariko, became Laura.)

Japanese farmworkers stayed mostly in boardinghouses during the winter. Some of the boarders were in the country illegally; others were legal but had secrets. There was a rumor at my grandmother's house that one boarder had been a bodyguard for a powerful man in Nagasaki. But when the powerful man was attacked and lost a limb, the bodyguard, who should have killed himself, moved to California, where he became a farmworker. A second man with a secret walked into my grandmother's house one day, looking for a room. It was the middle of summer. The place was empty, since everyone had a job during the summer and stayed at a farm camp.

The few available women in town, and even most of the married ones, immediately started to make excuses to drop by to see the second man, since he was very beautiful. The man was always mooning. Everyone figured he'd been in love in Japan but something had gone wrong.

One day, Obāsan bought a chicken she planned to kill and cook for my mother's birthday supper. Someone stole it one night, and later the next afternoon the smell of cooking chicken wafted out of the beautiful man's room. Anyway, Obāsan's kids said so; she wasn't home, and he denied everything.

Several women in town fell in love with him. And despite the stolen chicken, Obāsan's daughters liked him and would spy and giggle while he read in the living room. They fought over who got to give him his haircuts. That was my mother's chore, but her sisters paid her for the job. Even Obāsan's sons were curious: they wanted to grow up to be as mysterious as the beautiful man. Obāsan thought the man mooned too much—not her type. She knew this. Yet she was drawn to him, just like everyone else.

Meanwhile the house was falling apart, shifting in the ground. These are the sounds the house made: tick-tocking in the walls; thunder from below the floor; squeaks, scrapes, and groans from above. Sometimes as you lay in bed you might hear a plunk as a piece of the ceiling fell to the floor. Sometimes a piece of the ceiling might fall in bed beside you.

The house filled again when winter returned. Each house had its own personality, its own advantages to recommend it. For instance, there was one place that housed almost all boarders from the same prefecture in Japan, other places that allowed gambling and drinking. Some boarders chose "clean" houses, like my grandmother's, to live in, but went out frequently to gamble and drink at other establishments. Everyone in Obāsan's house played the board game Go—all the players sitting in one small room, all men, all with hair either silver or black. The players were intoxicated by the intensity in the room, by the stuffiness, by the soft sound of the sliding, shifting game pieces. The games went on hour after hour during winter evenings. While the men played, the kids crept through the room, pressing their ears against the walls and floor as they listened to the house's noises.

The beautiful man tried several times to get Obāsan to sleep with him, and she was tempted because at the time her husband was away and she felt lonely. Besides, she thought if you allowed yourself to choose what seemed wrong sometimes, you had more choices in the long run. But she didn't sleep with him. "Your conscience told you not to?" I once asked.

"No, my instinct," she said.

One night when her husband was back, he and the beautiful man got into a fight, and the man pulled a knife. Luckily, another boarder was watching and saved her husband. The boarder said that during the fight he'd noticed the man's face change for a second. It changed so much he was unrecognizable, but when the fight ended he looked like himself again. In any event, Obāsan almost lost her husband twice: the first time when the beautiful man tempted her to sleep with him (her husband would have left her if he found out); and the second time when he pulled the knife. Obāsan didn't figure out until years later that the beautiful man was the devil and was actually trying to take her husband from her. A few months later, he succeeded, when her husband drowned in Hawaii. They'd been married almost twenty years.

After the fight, in late spring, my grandparents kicked the man out. He was glad to go; he said he'd found a job picking cantaloupes. With the arrival of the picking season, all the boarders departed, leaving the house somber and quiet. My grandparents sold the house and worked in the fields a couple of months before moving to Hawaii. My grandmother said all the fields looked pretty much the same—flat, full of produce—but eventually she came to know each piece of land the way she knew the lay of her husband's body, each slope and angle and warm spot.

My brothers called this the murder story. I didn't tell it well, but it was their favorite.

✵ 5

✵✵ After Obāsan's funeral we started to drive south with the Shibatas. It had just gotten dark when Sam Shibata signaled us from behind to pull to the side. When we did, he parked his car in front of ours and walked toward us, squinting from the headlights. He told my father he'd had a premonition about an accident, and it was bad luck to continue now. We agreed to stop, because we always became superstitious traveling, the way a group of people isolated on an island might become superstitious. Somebody was always seeing a ghost or having a hunch or hearing a rumor. No idea had definite form; every fact could dissolve into fiction. "Too much magic on the road," Obāsan always said.

She was right. For instance, while we were searching for someplace to eat, everyone went crazy for a few minutes without seeming to realize it. My father turned around and boxed my ears, the way my grandmother always did, and my mother, who didn't smoke, lit a cigar of the type my grandmother favored. Peter sat in my lap. He grimaced strangely at me—the same sort of grimace Obāsan often made. He looked just like her, except he had even fewer teeth. I stared at him, not believing he could be making that face. Walker tapped me on the shoulder. He nodded sadly. "Too much magic on the road," he said.

In fact, an accident did occur that night, and it became part of my family's lore that Sam had predicted the future.

32

In all our time traveling, only two terrible things ever happened: my grandmother's death, and the accident, in which a bus hit a car. Because the death and the accident occurred within a few days of each other, I have always connected the two events.

My family and the Shibatas pulled into a cafeteria-bus stop for dinner. A couple of other kids were hanging around—they wore aprons, so I knew they worked there—and I offered them a few lemons. My family had picked some lemons up north, from a friend's tree. My brothers and I used to eat lemons like oranges or apples, or any other fruit.

The kids accepted my gift, and I had two new, temporary friends, a boy and a girl. "We've got to get to work in a second," said the girl.

"What do you do?"

"Bus coming," said the boy. His eyes bugged out as he took a bite of lemon.

"We clean off tables and stuff," said the girl.

"I'll help you for a quarter," I said.

"A nickel," said the boy and girl together.

"A dime."

"Deal," said the boy.

They paid me a nickel and said they'd give me the rest later. My parents always gave me money when I asked, but I didn't like to ask. I had inherited my grandmother's magic purse, though now it was always empty. I put my nickel inside.

The cafeteria was cozy. It smelled of french fries, and all the customers seemed to be developing thin layers of grease around their lips as they ate. Outside, it was dark; the reflections in the windows enclosed the cafeteria. My brothers ate some beef with glop on it. I ate a couple of lemons, then fruit salad on which I poured eleven packets of sugar. It ruined the fruit, but my grandmother never let me use much sugar, and I was testing my new freedom. My mother gave me a that's-bad-but-I'll-let-it-go-because-it's-been-a-hard-week look. I asked her where Obāsan's soul had gone to, heaven or hell.

"It didn't go to either one," she said. "It just sort of dispersed, so it's a little bit in everyone who knew her, more in some of us than others."

I didn't like the thought of my grandmother's soul inside me. It made me feel itchy. I started to get the feeling that a piece of her soul was inside my neck, and I couldn't stop scratching. I noticed Ben and Walker, across the table, twitching and squirming.

When the bus came, the cafeteria filled with customers, transforming the place. The reflections seemed to glisten with movement. A man fell asleep over his coffee at one table; I pointed out to my mother how a woman had just poured seven packets of sugar into her coffee; another woman stood in line, talking to herself.

When the bus driver called his passengers, I helped my friends clean up. "These plates look gross," I said.

"You get used to it," said the boy, plucking a french fry from a plate and biting into it.

I liked busing tables. I liked doing it the way I guess children like playing any role: baton twirler, shortstop, table cleaner. Anyway, that's what I was doing when the bus hit a car. The other thing I remember is catching the eye of a customer across the room. When I looked up at the sound of the crash—actually more like a big branch breaking than a crash—a strange almost-smile crossed his face: not a malicious smile, or even a conscious one, but a small, surprised smile. It didn't make sense, almost as if he were smiling because he was surprised he was smiling.

We all ran out in a very organized way. Each person waited patiently at the doorway for the next to get through, and when the person got out, he or she ran hard toward the accident. The part of our brains reserved for emergencies had come into play. It seemed that we'd expected the crash and knew just what to do, had in fact practiced all this just yesterday.

At first I ran as hard as I could, but at the sight of the bus I stopped, to take everything in. Way in the background, the moon was exactly over a hill. The moon didn't look flat the way it usually did. It looked spherical and close, like a globe sitting on top of the hill. Closer in, some men, including my father, were already trying to heave over the bus, which was lying door side down. The men were counting, "One, two, three," and then pushing. It wasn't until I got closer that I noticed a woman lying in the street. A number of people were assembled around her, like a gathering of trees or plants, moving only slightly, as with the wind. A couple of children were wailing, a few people were shouting orders. But I think that even if everyone had been crying out or running about, the woman's stillness would have made it seem a quiet moment. Someone laid a coat on her and said, "Don't worry, hon," again and again.

We had to wait for an ambulance from the next town. The man I'd noticed in the restaurant was still smiling. I would have thought he was the demon from my grandmother's stories, only he wasn't beautiful. Some of the kids who were crying—kids about my age—were sent inside by their parents. My two friends were sent in. Then the only kids left were older than I by a few years. I looked toward my parents, but they weren't noticing me. I felt suddenly, violently curious about the woman as she lay there. Sometimes I developed sudden passionate curiosities—I would need to acquire some fact or understanding or bit of knowledge, and felt I would die without it. It could be anything. I might need to see a house we'd lived in whose color I'd forgotten, or I might have seen a dead sparrow and want to know how long sparrows usually lived. Sometimes I got so upset if I couldn't know what I wanted that I think my parents were scared—I even felt scared myself at how hysterical I became. When they could, my parents took me to a library. But if we couldn't stop, or if I wanted to know something secret, my distress faded into a soft craving, a sort of ache, until finally I felt used and exhausted.

I moved across the broken glass, sort of darting forward, but then I got scared and darted quickly back. I did this a couple of times, arguing with myself. I thought it was wrong to look at the woman too closely, and tried to fight my curiosity. Then I darted forward again, but when I started to move backward, I ran into Walker. He'd sneaked up behind me and was staring at the woman. Later he told me I gasped when I saw him. "Don't look!" I said. "Get *outta* here fast." I felt I had to protect him from something. His whole body tensed against the imminent danger my voice seemed to warn him of. He buried his head against me for a moment, then looked up to check the traffic before running furiously to our car.

The bus sat upright now. The driver got back in and just sat there behind the wheel. I looked at the woman. A thin black stream trickled from her mouth. A couple of times she coughed, and we all stirred. Her arms and hands lay gracefully, as if specially arranged.

It took an hour for an ambulance to come. Meanwhile people debated passionately on whether they should move the woman themselves; my parents voted yes. I raised my hand to vote yes, but I was too young, and they didn't count me. We waited around even after the ambulance had left. The firemen came, and then a tow truck. There were still about thirty people waiting around. I don't know what we were waiting for. Once, a man said, "Guess they took her to Mercy," and a couple of people nodded. Another time, someone suggested, "We should get the mayor to put up more lights on the road." We all turned to look at the only light nearby, then we all turned to look at the bits of glass where the accident had been. I sat on a car with my mother, shivering. It had grown quite cool.

A woman began to tap nervously on another car, but in a couple of minutes the tapping became regular, a sort of heartbeat. Though it was getting late, the sky, which should have been black, had an eerie orange cast. I could feel my body swaying slightly to the beating. It seemed almost religious, or tribal, the way we all wanted to be together now, thinking about the woman who was hurt. My mother started to cry, something she hadn't done at Obāsan's funeral, and I knew she was crying not just for the woman but also for her mother.

The smiling man picked a flower from the side of the road

and gently laid it where the woman had been. He was so gentle I realized he wasn't evil. That was just my imagination.

After that we went to our car. When I sat down, my brothers looked eagerly at me, hoping I might tell them something they hadn't been able to see from the car. I didn't say anything. We searched for a motel with the Shibatas. Ben and Walker leaned against me, one on each shoulder, so I couldn't move or I would wake somebody up. That's a trivial thing, but it made me feel responsible for them, and a little lonely. I thought about how most of the people at the accident would probably find out what became of the woman, and because they would find out, they would care about her in a way that I wouldn't. I knew that a person had been hurt, maybe killed, yet to me the accident was already becoming something that had happened, *just* something that had happened, the way a fire we might pass on the road was just a fire we passed on the road, even though it was someone's house or farm burning. It was just part of Obāsan's floating world. There had been a couple of boys hanging around the accident. They might remember that night, at least a little bit, every time they walked by. This was probably bad for them, but also good. They would never have to brace themselves against all the things they couldn't know. And why couldn't my brothers be among those boys? That was one of the things I craved to understand.

✳✳ 6

✳✳ Nobody talked at all. I couldn't tell what my parents were thinking, or feeling. Sometimes I spent hours trying to figure them out, trying to make order of the random facts. My mother's body shook once, and I couldn't tell whether she was still crying or just had a chill.

My mother was thirty, tall, with a smooth face except for two furrows between her brows. She had a quiet, throaty voice I loved to listen to. Often my mother gave me advice I couldn't yet fathom. I remembered how, when I was seven, we passed a plot of opened morning glories. She pointed at them. "That's the way you'll feel inside the first time a boy you love touches you." Later we passed the same flowers, closed into tight little twists. "And that," she said, "is how you'll feel inside the first time a boy you don't love touches you."

The only grandparent I knew well was Obāsan. My father's parents had left the United States when he was a teenager. They'd joined a religion based in Kyoto. The leader of the religion had been an eleven-year-old girl who said she spoke with God. When she got old and died, her younger brother and sister both said they now spoke with God, and they took over the religion.

I was born in Fresno, where my mother lived. My father, or the man I have always thought of as my father, lived in Oregon before he married my mother. I was not that much smaller than he. He was five feet three, and his name was Charles Osaka—Charlie-O to everyone except my mother, who called him Charles when she didn't like him and Chuck when she did, just as she called me Olivia or Livvie, depending on my behavior. Charlie-O was almost always cheerful, and he had a childlike joie de vivre that would not quite have fit a larger man. Obāsan forced my mother to marry him, though I wasn't supposed to know that. I'd picked it up over the years.

I don't know exactly how my grandmother found Charlie-O, but I later heard she'd first brought him to Fresno to meet my mother when she was seven months pregnant with me. My father used to keep a picture on his bureau of my mother on prom night, when she was seventeen, and sometimes I wonder whether that was the picture Obāsan first sent him to get him to Fresno. He married my mother when she was eight months pregnant, and in time they had my three brothers. I knew that Charlie-O loved me, though once in a while I worried that he loved me because I was what had brought him together with my mother. My real father visited me several times, but he was married and had two children, and we never became close. So I was devoted to Charlie-O and had followed him everywhere when I was quite young—he even took me to his poker games—and sometimes I brought him to Parents' Day at school, where, starting the past year, he was shorter than a couple of my classmates. But I was already beginning not to care about poker games and Parents' Days, and Charlie-O and I were growing apart. That hurt him. My allegiances were shifting to my mother. She was moody, but also graceful and pensive and intellectual, things I wanted to be when I grew up but already knew I never would be. Charlie-O was loud, undignified.

We'd lived in Florence, Oregon, for the past few months, and I think for a while my parents wanted to settle down. Charlie-O loved it there. He was an amateur painter, and sometimes, when my brothers or my grandmother and I went for walks not long after first light, Charlie-O would already be outside, painting on the beach. But when his friend offered him half a garage for a small down payment, he couldn't resist. Most of the Japanese where we were moving in Arkansas were chicken sexers, and I think my father sort of liked the idea of going there as a business owner. "Of course, I won't let it go to my head," he said. He told me that in Arkansas his friend sometimes met people who hadn't known that any Japanese lived in the state, although all the Japanese knew of one another.

In any case, in the car after the accident, my mother was the first to break the silence. She declared in her throaty voice that she had just decided she wanted to find Obāsan's second husband—her own second father. She hadn't seen him for nearly twenty years. I could tell that my mother felt obsessive about finding him. She was like that now and then—obsessive. But my dad didn't want to take the time. He didn't even want to stop off in Los Angeles to visit anymore. He was getting more and more excited about the garage, and we were already behind schedule.

My mother had sent her second father—Bill—a telegram about the funeral. He hadn't shown up or responded, though she thought he still lived in the same place where she'd lived with him—central California, about fifty miles from Wilcox. He was twenty years older than my grandmother, which would have made him ninety-six at the time of her death. As my mother talked about finding him, my father caught my eye in the rearview mirror, and I knew he thought Bill was probably dead. My mother read his mind. "Don't even think it," she said.

My mother talked about her fathers. When her first father died, she'd just turned seven, but she didn't remember a great deal about him, except that the last thing he'd said to her was "Be good." Her third father died, of old age, after a long marriage to her mother. But my mother hadn't liked him, and he hadn't liked her. In between, Bill had been her father. I thought it was great fun to hear all this.

After a short silence, my mother told us that Obāsan hadn't loved Bill, but she herself had. "Drop me off somewhere.

I'm going to take a bus and find him. Honey, can you stop the car?'' she said to Charlie-O. She jiggled the door handle. I looked into the bushes on either side of the car.

"You can't get out here," said my father. "And where will you stay when you get to this town?''

"At a motel?" she said. "At a motel.'' She sat up very straight, what she always did when she was ready to fight for something.

I didn't know a lot, but I knew that ladies did not stay in motels alone. My father sat up straight, too—he wasn't going to change *his* mind, either. My mother slumped a little. "It's always nice when we start out somewhere, then it's less nice when we're almost there,'' she said.

It was raining very hard. Walker pulled my ear down to his mouth and whispered. I tapped my father's shoulder. "Walker says we've lost the Shibatas.''

Charlie-O pulled over in a few minutes and made three announcements: first, he believed we were somewhere in Ventura County; second, he believed we were lost; and third, we were about to run out of gas.

"How do you know we're in Ventura County if we're lost?'' I said.

"Don't worry, honey-dog. You look worried.'' He smiled, but his eyes didn't look happy in the rearview mirror. His eyes looked uncertain and seemed to be asking me something— nothing specific; just asking.

I got out a map. "Where's the highway?'' I said.

He didn't know. The rain formed rivers down the windshield, and the raindrops made the windows look like textured glass. Charlie-O got out, and I pressed my nose against the backseat window and watched him squint into the darkness as the rain splashed on his face. He was looking down the road, but I didn't see why he couldn't look from inside the dry car. It was as if he were under a spell. I lowered the window. The air was warmer than I'd expected.

"Dad, what are you doing?''

"Just seeing what's what,'' he said. "I'm gonna walk down a ways and try to get us some gas.'' As he set off, he appeared as sturdy as always but even smaller than usual. I rolled up the window and ran after him, almost slipping in the mud as I hurried. Charlie-O walked on surefootedly.

"Why am I doing this?" I said. "I should just wait in the car."

We went a long way but never thought of turning back. We were both very stubborn. We'd always been alike that way. There was nothing but bush around us, and sometimes—maybe it was the play of sky light off the rain—I would think I saw lights in the leaves. Charlie-O didn't look either right or left as he walked, and I thought how much more scared I would be without him. He stopped, and I bumped into him. He was looking at three huge, beautiful signs hanging in the darkness beyond a hill. The signs were bright reds and blues and yellows: Standard, Shell, Motor Inn.

My father bought gas and suggested I wait at the station while he took the long walk back to the car. I stood under the awning while the attendant talked on the phone inside. Lightning kept illuminating the area beyond this enclave of two gas stations and a motel. When it flashed, the surrounding area looked not quite there, like a photographic negative. It seemed to take forever for my family to come.

Ben cringed from me when I got in the car. "You're all wet," he said, as if my wetness were a contagious disease.

"Just a little water," boomed Charlie-O. "Ain't nothing to have a cow about."

Usually when his voice sounded loud and happy that way, it was because he really felt loud and happy. But he was wet and tired, and though he was the one who'd decided we should leave Oregon, I thought about how much he'd liked it there, and how important it must be to him to have a success in Arkansas.

We drove across to the motel. I'd heard my parents say the day before that they would take two rooms tonight—one for my brothers and me, and one for themselves. I knew it was so they could make love. Only a couple of years earlier, I wouldn't have understood completely why it was so important for them to get their own room, as they sometimes did.

A tired-looking man with rollers in his hair registered us at the motel. When I watched my parents at the counter, they seemed to be the same person. Maybe it was just that they lived in the same world, used the same shampoo, ate the same foods. In any case, they matched. Yet I knew that sometimes my mother felt lonely and my father felt alone. And though my mother was several years younger than Charlie-O, she always struck me as womanly, whereas my father was boyish.

"One room?" said the man.

"Yes, plus cots, if you have any," said my mother.

The man got a cot. "Only have one. I won't charge you. We usually charge a dollar, but I understand. I've got seven of my own." A cry came from a back room. "There's one now," the man said with a sigh. He yawned and shook his head, and a loose roller jiggled.

Charlie-O turned and winked at me, and when we got outside he said, "Remember—you can always trust a man with seven children and the nerve to wear rollers in his hair." Charlie-O carried the cot to the room. Then he and I went to a coffee shop, where he got coffee and I stole packets of sugar and containers of ersatz cream to give my brothers. They were too young to be out so late.

When we got to our room, my mother was pensive, and I knew she was thinking again about finding her second father. Walker, Ben, and I played cards on the floor. Walker always beat Ben and me at poker, because he wouldn't change expressions, even when he had a good hand.

This time my father seemed to read my mother's mind. "We need to get to Arkansas. We've got to get them settled." I looked up. "Them" meant us—the kids.

My father leaned back against a bureau, smoking. His left forearm rested across his ribs, his right elbow sat on the back of his hand. To draw on his cigarette, he moved his right wrist downward to inhale and flipped it back up when he finished his drag. His elbow and head never moved. Then he tossed his hair back, as if waking himself, and became alert, interested. "Driving's okay sometimes, you know. You get a chance to think."

"What do you like to think about?" said my mother.

"About you," he said.

Cool, moist air wafted through the screen door. Outside, the reflections from the motel lights made flashing ribbons of color on the wet parking lot ground. A traveler entered the motel office, and in a few minutes he came out, keys jangling, and walked across the ribbons. The NO lit up in the vacancy sign.

My father was the most tired, from driving, and he, Walker, and Ben went to sleep. Peter stayed up. My mother and I leafed through a book called *Man of Steel*. To sustain my reading ability when we were moving, my mother always picked up what books she could find. While other children were reading *Lassie Come Home* and *The Call of the Wild*, I was reading *Reptiles and Amphibians: Nature's Throwbacks* or *Innards: How to Cook Variety Meats*. Actually, I gained a lot of knowledge. But I knew I didn't read as well as most people my age, and maybe I never would. I read out loud now: "Andrew Carnegie was a man with ideas." When my mother thought of it, she made me read twenty pages at a time, but I would see she wasn't listening tonight. I closed the book. "Do you think we'll like Arkansas?" I said. I thought she might want to talk.

She smiled, just barely, and shook her head yes. "What do you think?"

"Well." I wanted to sound wise. "If we don't, we can always leave."

She went to bed. Peter was quiet but wide awake. I took him out with me and sat on the curb. The wind blew hard against the lone tree in the distance. It was very dark, but you could see the roads crisscrossing over the fields. When cars went by, far away, the beams were so bright they seemed to be ropes of light pulling the cars behind.

My mother wanted badly to go and find Bill; my father wanted to get to Arkansas. I wished we didn't have to do anything. I wanted to stay where we were—where I didn't know anyone and no one knew me, and where it seemed to me a long time ago that my grandmother had died.

Back in the room, the lights were off, and everyone was asleep—my parents on the bed and my brothers wrapped like cocoons on the floor. You couldn't see their breathing movements; occasional twitches indicated that the moths inside might be emerging in a few hours or days. I had taught my brothers to wrap themselves up that way. We each used to have our own blanket, which we would fold in half before tucking in every inch under our bodies, including our heads. So long as you didn't thrash in your dreams, you could stay warm, even if it got quite cool during the night. I laid Peter between Ben and Walker. I wondered why my mother had decided to take just one room. Did it mean my parents weren't getting along, in ways I couldn't see? Everything changed so quickly and without my noticing.

I thought I remembered a time when my parents had been unable to keep their hands off each other, always walking arm in arm or stopping to kiss lightly. But the memory was there and then not there. One night on the way down from Oregon we'd taken only one motel room, but my parents had made love anyway quietly probably after they thought we were all asleep. I thought they'd *had* to make love or they wouldn't have—not with me and my brothers in the room. They'd never made love in the past when we'd taken only one room. Something about their lovemaking that night, about the sound of it, seemed somehow hopeless. I'd had to go to the bathroom badly, but by the time they finally fell asleep and I could get up, I'd decided that if necessary I would wet my bed before letting them know I was awake. It was not the sex I thought I ought not to have heard but the hopelessness.

I was on the cot, and my eyes were closed. I heard my mother and Charlie-O begin speaking, though I couldn't hear what they were saying. Finally she said something, and my father didn't answer. I heard the sheets rustle. I thought they were going to make love, but they didn't. Then they did. I opened my eyes and saw their bodies moving beneath the

sheets. I felt guilty for watching, so I closed my eyes again
and averted my face. But I couldn't help listening closely;
they were almost as silent as when they slept.

Afterward, my mother said, "It doesn't make any sense,"
and my father concurred. I had no idea *what* didn't make any
sense. I'm not even sure they knew, yet it seemed like the
right thing to say. Sometimes I worried that my parents were
disappointed with their lives, and I wondered how much of
that might be due to my brothers and me—maybe we weren't
the kind of children they'd hoped for. But I thought I would
rather they be unhappy with me than with each other. Of
course, that wasn't the case—despite our faults, my parents
couldn't have been happier with my brothers and me.

My parents fell asleep. The cot squeaked softly as I shook
my feet up and down, back and forth. I lay still and realized
Walker wasn't breathing evenly—he was awake. The others
were asleep. Walker had probably heard our parents making
love. I wished he hadn't. It seemed to me a burden to have
heard, and I didn't want him to have that burden.

"Walk?" I said.

"Huh."

"Good night."

He didn't answer, but I knew he felt comforted not to be
alone, and soon he fell asleep. So did I. Maybe I felt comforted, too.

The next day we headed back north. I first knew what we
were doing shortly after my father drew out the map and
placed it on the car hood. My mother studied the map over
his shoulder, then suddenly said, "You know it's okay if you
all don't come," and my father replied by making a cere-
mony of folding up the map and getting into the car.

We arrived in Bill's town that evening. The town had a
miniature mall on the main street. My mother said there used
to be several separate shops on the street, but now the shops
were housed in adjoining buildings, all with the same white-
and-blue facades. When we reached Bill's road, a detour
blocked the way. "It's not far—ten or fifteen minutes' walk-

ing," my mother said. She was very excited. "If you want, you can let me out and pick me up later." But my father turned off the ignition and got out, and we set off.

The houses were spread out, almost as in farm country. At one time, my mother said, there had been no houses except hers in this area.

"Did I used to live here?" said Ben. He gestured hugely at the fields around us.

"No. Mom lived here a long time ago," I said.

"Will you give me a piggyback ride?"

"You're getting kind of big."

He sighed. "I know."

The lights from the downtown shops, beyond a hill, shone at the horizon, making the ground seem to glow. When we reached my mother's old address, the house was dark, and my mother hesitated, then peeked into a window on the door. The door opened as she was peeking, and she took a step back. An old woman stood at the threshold. This would be Bill's wife. My mother, beautiful, smiled her most charming smile, and the woman's suspicious face softened, but only a little. "I sent a telegram" was all my mother said.

"Yes," said the woman. The suspicion returned. She and my mother stood, waiting. "You see, he has been dead for quite a while."

I think she expected us to say good-bye then, but my mother just stood there, and after a pause the woman let us in. It was cool outside but even cooler inside, as if the blinds had not been raised all day, and I had the feeling that the house had few visitors. The woman turned on a light. The living room was oppressively orange: the carpet was orange, the couch had orange-and-brown flowers, and the curtains were pasty orange. Probably the woman thought orange was a cheerful color; therefore, the more orange the better. The house smelled of ginger—a mix of fresh ginger and stale.

When the woman showed us around, my mother saw a pair of children's shoes sitting in a sewing room. "Oh, those are mine!" she said.

The woman looked as if she'd been accused. "Did you

want them back?'' She looked doubtfully at my mother's feet, then at mine, which were big.

Back in the living room, my mother found something else she thought belonged to her—an enameled box of the kind her mother used to make. She thought it was the same one her mother had given her for her tenth birthday. The woman seemed offended and said Bill had given it to her, but she was sure he'd bought it. When she left to get refreshments, my mother said, ''I know that's my box. I loved that box. I always wondered what happened to it.''

I piped up. ''It sure looks like the other ones she used to make.'' Sometimes my mouth opened even when I didn't want it to.

My father said, ''Let's not stay long.''

When the woman returned, she talked mainly to my brothers and me. She told us how, when she first came to this country from Japan, she'd been a farmworker and picked tomatoes. The tomato plants smelled like marigolds, and now she couldn't stand that smell. I loved the scent of marigolds, and I couldn't imagine things happening in my life that would make me hate it. But I couldn't be sure.

While the woman talked I saw something strange. My mother, with that familiar obsessive look on her face, was trying to get the enameled box into her handbag, but Charlie-O had hold of her wrist, and his face was just as determined as hers. I looked at my brothers, but they hadn't noticed anything.

The woman continued to talk, and I asked her question after question while out of the corner of my eye I watched my parents struggle. They were so intent I doubt they would have noticed if we'd all turned to watch. I half expected to see them fall to the floor, wrestling. My father, of course, won. But my mother's face caved in, and I could see that a part of Charlie-O wanted to let her have the box.

Later, when everyone else was saying good-bye, I surprised myself by meandering over and slipping the box into my jacket pocket. I think I had an idea that giving it to my mother would please both my parents—my mother because she would get the box and not have to tell my father, and my father because my mother would be content, though he wouldn't know why.

When we left and the woman closed the door, the lights went off almost immediately. The woman seemed to have come to life just for us. My mother called me over to a window, and we peeked in. "What do you see?" she said.

I stared. I squinted. I tried to imagine. Finally I said, "Nothing."

She nodded sagely. "That's what I see." I thought she was still a little crazy from her mother dying.

All around I could hear the noise of dry grass riffling like paper. My father was standing right behind us, waiting, but my mother kept her face pressed to the window. "Your father's mad because he had to come all the way out here," she said. "But he didn't have to come."

I didn't answer. Though she said "your father," she was really talking to him.

"I wanted to come," he said. "I'm not mad." He shouted to Ben and Walker, "Get back here now!" Ben and Walker had been running across the road. "Watch them," he said to me.

I turned to look at them play in the empty road, then turned back to my parents. My father leaned against the house and closed his eyes and opened them again, as if he thought the world would have changed when he reopened his eyes. I peeked back inside. Maybe what my mother saw in there was something like what I would see, years from then, when I looked back on that night. I heard my brothers playing and laughing behind me but didn't hear a sound from my parents. Peter was quiet but wide-eyed in my mother's arms.

"What do you want?" said Charlie-O, very quietly.

"I don't want anything," my mother said.

"You don't understand—I want you to want something."

"I just don't want you to be mad," my mother said to the window. A small steam circle formed on the glass where she was talking. I felt very old suddenly, because I knew she'd only said that for him. What she'd said first was closer to the truth: she didn't want anything he could give her.

"I'm not mad," Charlie-O said. "Maybe we can find a sitter or something. Maybe we should go get plastered or something."

We left, my parents walking hand in hand. I didn't look back at the house, but I thought I felt the woman's eyes on my back. She was going to run out any second and reclaim her enameled box. I already knew I would never give it to my mother; she would be disappointed that I'd taken it. One of these days I was going to try to be good for a whole week.

I could see now that no gain or lack of a box was going to change my mother's life any. She'd probably already forgotten about it. I ran back to the house and placed the box carefully on the doorstep, then ran back to catch up with my family. My mother was walking ahead now. No one even asked me why I'd run back. It was getting so you could do any nutty thing and no one else would even notice.

"Why is Mom walking ahead?" said Walker to my father.

"She's thinking. It's okay."

"What's she thinking about?"

"Walker is practically having a conversation," said Ben. "He never talks."

"She's thinking about things."

"What things?"

"I can see the car," said Ben. "Livvie, I'll race you." But then he ran to a fence to look at a rabbit he thought he'd spotted.

"But is she happy up there? Is she lonely or happy? And is she thinking about Obāsan?" said Walker.

"About your grandmother, and maybe other things," Charlie-O said. "She's lonely but also happy."

"How come both?"

My father hesitated, figuring. "She's lonely because she had too many fathers, and happy because that's never going to happen to you. I didn't come all the way out here to be mad."

The lights from downtown had all been turned off, and the

ground no longer seemed to glow. Darkness intensified every noise—our footsteps, our voices. I thought of how a couple of months earlier my mother had told my brothers and me about our "stars"—the word she used for the personality traits she thought would make our lives easier. One night, as she and I were sitting looking over a grove of plum trees, she lowered her voice, as if she had a great secret, and said she had finally figured out what my star was, what I had that would ease my way through the future. It wasn't Peter's alertness, or Walker's concentration, or Ben's self-assurance. But I had a happy heart—my birthright, she said. I sat leaning my head against her shoulder, hoping that someday my happy heart would take me to the right places, get me the right jobs, let me love the right man. Then I wondered whether her mother had ever told her that she had a happy heart, and I asked her the same question I asked my father now: "Did you just make a wish, or a promise?"

7

※※ We passed in and out of alertness while we traveled. Late one morning while we drove through endless fields of yellow flowers, suddenly one or two purple flowers appeared. I sat up. Sometimes a sudden new color made me alert. In a minute there were scattered bursts, then waves, of purple. We were quiet.

I wondered whether I would ever be a secretary, as I'd dreamed at Isamu's. My mother had had three jobs, all in high school: typist, seamstress, maid. She met my real father because his sister worked as a maid in the house next door to where my mother worked. So that job affected her whole life. As for her seamstress skills, she used those all the time, mending our clothes. But after her high school job, she used a typewriter only once. At the end of one year, when I had to return an artbook to the school library, I got very depressed. I had fallen in love with the book. Obāsan, naturally, wanted to steal the book, but Charlie-O wouldn't hear of it. So for a surprise my mother borrowed a typewriter and typed up my favorite chapters. She didn't know that what I loved most was not the text but the pictures. Still, I kept the manuscript she'd typed in my collection of special things. Other items I kept were some candy; the strand from my grandmother's braid; a prize I won in third grade for throwing a softball the second farthest of the girls in my class; and a silver button that was the only thing Obāsan ever gave me. Sometimes as we drove I sat and looked over my special things, examining each one.

The surrounding fields were filled with purple flowers. It was time to stop for lunch.

We were in bad spirits later. From around three to five was usually the worst time. We were often hot, and tired of driving. All six of us were in a terrible mood at once that day. We stopped at a crossing because a train was coming. But it moved so slowly! My father, usually the most good-natured, pounded the steering wheel with impatience. As the engine passed us, my brothers and I leaned out the windows, waving and shouting "Hi" to the three men in the engine. "Say Hi back," screamed Ben. "What's wrong? Are you guys deaf? I hate you. *Say Hi*." The engine passed, and then the whole train halted.

"Oh, now what. We're going to be here all day," said my father.

The train backed up. Three men sitting in the engine pondered us. "Uh-oh," said Ben. "Duck—they're going to shoot." Peter ducked. The men smiled and waved. One of them yelled "Cute kids" to my mom. Then the train moved forward. My brothers and I were amazed—we had stopped a whole train. After that, we were all in better spirits. My brothers and I behaved for the rest of the afternoon. The noise inside the car was soothing and constant, like the breath of the sea in a shell.

We passed in and out of alertness while we traveled.

8

✵ The day we planned to arrive in Arkansas, we got up early. We'd spent the night in a motel in Texas. All of us felt very excited—not exactly optimistic, just excited. Ben jabbered relentlessly all day. He kept socking my arm to get my attention as he viewed the arid landscape. "Where are the people, I ask you?" Walker just stared, sometimes at the back of the front seat.

My mother, as she sometimes did, had Ben, Walker, and me get out and run until we were exhausted, so we wouldn't beat up on each other so much in the car. Over the distant plains, hundreds of kites were flying. They looked like confetti in the sky. Above them, the clouds were soft and flesh-colored, like a baby. My mother said maybe there was a kite contest or a marathon going on. When we left, we all stuck our heads out the window and watched until we couldn't see the confetti any longer.

The big thing that went wrong on this part of the trip was we lost Walker for a few hours. He climbed under a tarpaulin in the back of a pick-up during our lunch break, and the owner accidentally drove off with him. Walker had a habit of wandering off. He wasn't trying to run away. He would just see something that interested him and go off to look at it. Then he stayed to daydream, or else fell asleep or wandered off once more. We had to drive back almost three hours to retrieve him, but he didn't get scolded. That was the thing

about Walker. He was so thin and quiet we all felt we needed
to take care to be gentle with him, even as he worried us.
Though we were six hours behind schedule, my parents decided we should try to make Arkansas without another overnight stop.

My father was tired, so my mother took over the driving.
We drove until very late. At times there were no streetlights
or billboards, no other vehicles on the road. Once, a truck
from the opposite direction started out as a single pinpoint
of light, then grew into two pinpoints. As it closed in, the
brightness of the headlights against the highway's darkness
created the illusion that the truck was bearing down on us,
in our own lane. "Watch it!" my father said, and my mother
braked hard to pull over. When the truck passed, in its own
lane, the driver tooted his horn; my mother tooted back.

The sudden braking woke all three of my brothers. Outside, there was a small light above a rest-stop sign, and a
swarm of gnats darkened the light. Peter blinked at the light
and sat up straight, already wide awake though it was 2:30
A.M. I wondered whether he would remember this someday.
My own earliest memories were of pictures from a car window—telephone wires illuminated by streetlamps, factories
outlined against a still, sunless sky—pictures of one world
fading as another took its place. The gnats were already dis-
appearing as my mother accelerated onto the road.

My father turned on the light and started to read a map. It
annoyed my mother to drive with the light on, though she
didn't say so now. The car seemed to be filling with tension.
A station wagon came from the opposite direction, then made
a U-turn over a divider, and I felt a brief chill, as if the car
were chasing us. But it sped on.

Ben was examining a wet spot on his shirt, where Peter
apparently had drooled. "You drooled on me!" said Ben.

"No I didn't!"

"I want you to stop this discussion before it starts," said
my mother.

"Can I open a window back here?" I said.

"It's late," said my mother shortly. Walker was sitting

face backward, watching the road unwind behind us. I turned to see. The clouds looked like long, ragged scrapes across the sky. When I turned forward again, my father was shaking a fist in the air. "It's going to be *fine* in Arkansas," he said, as if one of us had suggested otherwise. Peter had fallen back asleep, and he *was* drooling. Walker climbed in front and fell asleep between our parents. After a while my father turned off the car light.

"Good night," I said.

"Good night," said my parents. They both sounded surprised that I hadn't fallen asleep yet.

With the light off, the tension seemed to escape through the cracks between the windows and doors, easing out into the dark. I imagined it on the roadside now, waiting. I fell asleep, and when I woke again the Ozarks were swelling on the horizon. I forced myself to stay awake and watch while we drove through the Ozarks, where fogs were rising like smoke rings around the hills. From one high spot I could see the clock over the Gibson Bank, telling time to the sleeping houses. That was our new town—Gibson. I was surprised to see a red-orange stain in a corner of the dark sky. It was spreading almost perceptibly. As we drove through Gibson, the town seemed strangely dry in lush surroundings. Dirt and rock dominated the small highway that ran through town, and asphalt and metal dominated the large one. Along the large highway the smooth geometrical shapes of factories rose behind the gas stations, groceries, and boarded-up firecracker stands. The residential roads were mostly dirt, with old tires and rusted cars seeming to sit on every dirt lawn in front of every small frame house. I wasn't disappointed. I was too tired for that. I was just glad we'd arrived someplace.

We all slept until noon on the living room floor of the house we were renting, and then we looked around. The house was old and roomy, with sprawling yards outside and a huge dark basement below. When we first went downstairs our voices seemed to dissolve in the empty room, the musty air sopping up the sound. In the living room, a number of nail holes from old hangings dotted the walls, and with each breeze, dust mice came to life in the room's corners. I reserved judgment about the house. Sometimes I hated our houses at first, then later hated leaving them.

The first thing my mother did was unpack a picture of Obāsan. In front of the picture she placed a water glass—a shot glass, actually—and filled it with water so Obāsan wouldn't get thirsty. It was my job to see that my grandmother always had a fresh bowl of rice set next to the water. On New Year's, my mother said, we would give her some sweet-bean pastries, her favorite dessert. I vowed to do a good job taking care of my grandmother, and someday, I knew, I would tell my mother how I had killed her.

My life seemed less frantic without Obāsan, yet I also felt more vulnerable: through attrition, we were a weaker family now. I dreamed I told my mother about the night of Obāsan's death and she didn't feel I'd killed anyone. "My mother was a guilty woman. She told me once she felt guilty about the way she treated you, and about other things from her life. My mother was also frugal. She didn't believe anything should be wasted. She gave you her boxes, her fans, her pictures, your memories of her nice walks. The night she decided to die, she gave you her guilt. Use it." She thought that over and added, "Of course, you were very bad and deserve to be guilty."

After her initial grief, my mother had become more meditative than sad. Years ago, we'd had very few possessions we couldn't carry in a car, but this trip we'd needed a small trailer. My mother was responsible for all the unpacking, though we helped. I think she felt both affection and resentment toward our possessions. No matter how hard she tried to stanch the growth of the number of things we owned, we seemed to be accumulating more and more. At times she seemed to feel that soon her life would be ruled and defined by our pink kitchen chairs, the embroidered bedspreads she'd made, the stained kitchen towels. "Watch out for life," Obāsan used to say. "It's harder than it looks." My mother had taken this to heart—she'd always been waiting for that second banana peel, that gargantuan slipup that would send her life sprawling. The other banana peel was my real father. When she first moved to Arkansas, I think she was starting to feel that from here her life would be a slow climb either up, down, or nowhere.

Arkansas was humid, and the clouds at night were unnaturally white, as if someone had spilled bleach on the black sky. I liked to sit late in the backyard, and in bed each night my arms and legs would be covered with mosquito bites, some of them as big and round as quarters, others longer, thinner, like welts. We lived near the outside of Gibson, in one of a cluster of old houses close to some hills. My father was a big believer in organizations, and he joined a bowling team, a golf club, and a group of small-business owners, which was really sort of a poker club. His friend he owned the garage with did most of the office work, while my father did most of the garage work, but Charlie-O was still proud to be a business owner. He subscribed to a business newsletter, and whenever he was reading it we would all have to be very quiet around the house.

I met some of the children of my parents' new friends, but most of them lived in other towns, and though I liked the kids from my class, school had never interested me, and that didn't change in Arkansas. There was a boy I liked from the next town. I didn't think he liked me, but just his being there made me hopeful for a future as lush as I lately imagined my mother's past—I knew she'd loved my real father a great deal, and I thought she loved Charlie-O. My mother was amused by my crush. ''You forget everything so easily when you're young,'' she said, referring to a boy I'd liked in Oregon. She was right about him but wrong about my memory. There were many things I remembered. For instance, I remembered how my grandmother had frequently told me that if I hoped to get what I wanted in the future, I would always have to take great care with what meager looks I had. At night I would take off my clothes and stand on the rim of the bathtub so I could see my body in the medicine-cabinet mirror. But I knew that if I didn't get what I wanted in life it wouldn't be because my skin was not the smoothest, or my hair not the blackest and straightest. I knew that much about my future.

The first time I spent more than a few minutes with the boy I liked was about half a year after we'd arrived, when Charlie-O and my mother were driving him, his parents, and me to a party—children were always invited to the parties of my parents' new friends. I sat next to the boy in the car, and I was nervous and chewing my fingernails. Charlie-O laughed and said, "I remember when you were little you used to chew your toenails."

I felt mortified, but the boy didn't seem to have heard. I slunk down in my seat.

Charlie-O continued: "And then after you'd bit them off you used to swallow them."

I considered flinging myself out of the car to my death, but we were going only thirty miles an hour, and I probably would have just got a concussion. I looked at the boy and he smiled, and for the first time I thought he might like me.

Charlie-O had just resumed his art interest, and on Saturdays he would take me when he went painting landscapes. In Oregon I never went painting with him, though he asked all of us to. Since I'd decided that he and I weren't close any longer, perhaps it was two-faced of me to make such a turn-around, here where I had few friends and needed company—any company.

He was not a good painter. He painted pictures of forests, with solid yellow sunbeams plunging through the trees like missiles from heaven, and his clouds were applied in thick globs, "for texture." But it was fun to go painting, anyway. My brothers and I owned a microscope, and I would take it along and examine insects, blades of grass, whatever I came upon. Other times, I painted. Charlie-O showed me how to hold a brush—not like a pencil but the way you would hold a brush to paint a house. That, he said, was how the Impressionists held brushes.

Though his paintings were awful, he hung them up in the garage and offered them for sale. Sometimes he painted me and my brothers, and he hung up those pictures, as well.

Once, when I stopped by the garage, he told a customer he'd painted pictures of all his children. The customer pointed to a portrait of Peter. "Is that you?" she said to me.

"That's my brother," I said. I paused. I wanted to defend Charlie-O. "My father does great likenesses, but my brother and I look a *lot* alike. People *always* get us mixed up."

Charlie-O momentarily looked confused. "I didn't know people always mixed you up," he said. Whenever he heard me tell a lie, he believed me at first, even if he should have known I was lying. That's how much he trusted me.

"Have you ever sold a painting?" I asked him after the customer left.

"Oh, sure," he said. He winked and pointed to his head with his forefinger. "I've sold lots of paintings." In his imagination, he meant.

We'd all got used to Arkansas in a hurry. Though we lived out of the way, relatives visited us now and then with their families. When my family was out with a relative's family, you always felt people were staring if you weren't looking. There were no blacks living in Gibson; only whites and the few Japanese. We were all very quiet in public.

When we moved there, Gibson was small—a few thousand people—but spread out, so across town could be as much as seven miles at certain points. We had thought of moving to a town called Ashland, but no Japanese lived there, and we didn't want to be the first. My father said that the fourteen Japanese, including the six of us, who lived in Gibson all came from families who owned small businesses, and the twenty or thirty Japanese in the next town over, Lee (for Robert E. Lee), all came from families in which someone worked as a chicken sexer. But no chicken sexers lived in Gibson, and no business-owner Japanese lived in Lee. I don't know why it was divided that way.

My mother was always busy. Since I had turned thirteen, old enough to stay alone with my brothers, she wanted to get a job; my father, however, didn't approve. So she joined a church, not because she was religious but because she wanted to learn. She went to the library every day some weeks. My mother read a lot in a community where men rarely—and women never—read books. A couple of times at parties, I watched the women scurry back and forth cleaning up as the men dropped nutshells on the carpet and ashes on the coffee table. When the women went into the kitchen to clean, my mother remained in the living room to talk, and I felt faintly ashamed, and unsure whether I ought to stay in the living room or go into the kitchen. Usually I stayed in the living room, but I didn't really talk to anyone. So I never had to help clean up.

More than a year after we moved to Arkansas, I found out my mother had had an affair when we lived in Oregon. I walked into the living room one day and came upon Charlie-O and my mother standing in the center of the room, doing nothing, saying nothing. I hadn't heard any shouting, but something in the room felt the way it did after a big fight in the house. Peter had been peeking out the window, but he turned when he heard me walk in. He appeared pleased to see me.

"What's going on?" I said.

"There's a man out there, waiting for Mom."

My parents still didn't move, and I went to the window. On the walkway stood a man I'd seen around in Florence, Oregon—a friend of my mother's. At first I didn't know why he was out there, why he didn't come in. Charlie-O went outside to talk to him. While my mother waited, her hands started shaking. We stared at the hands. It seemed as if someone else, someone invisible, were shaking them. I thought about how my grandmother's soul was inside all of us. So for a second I didn't know whether it was my grandmother inside my mother, shaking the hands, or whether something was physically wrong with my mother. My own body also seemed to hold revelations more profound than I could grasp. My face flushed and my stomach grew tense, and then I understood who the man was: my mother's lover.

"Who is it?" whispered Peter. Though young, he had an instinctive ability to detect when something had gone wrong.

"The enemy," I whispered back. I suddenly hated that man. "Remember, Peter," I whispered fiercely, "if you ever see that man, he's the *enemy.*" Peter looked scared, and I wished I hadn't spoken.

When Charlie-O came in, the man left. The house was extra quiet. My parents went into the bedroom to talk. I worked with our microscope. I studied dust, hair, lake water, spit. As I stared at amoebae, I kept thinking of a fight I'd overheard a few weeks before we left Oregon. My mother had been crying, and she said, "I tell you I *am* grateful. But now—do you still want me?" Charlie-O said he didn't know. "I don't know if you *should* still want me," she said. "And I don't know if I want you to."

We were all supposed to go to a party later—it was a local novelist's birthday—though I figured now we wouldn't go. But after a while my parents came out of their room and told us we were leaving in half an hour. I went through the house to the front porch. Sometimes Obāsan used to make my brothers and me sit on the front porch for a long time as punishment. Now and then she locked the front door, but that was just for show, since no matter where we lived, the back door was never locked, even when we left the house, and if I really wanted to come in I could just walk around back. I hardly ever did, though; I actually liked sitting outside alone.

Hills in the distance blocked out part of the sky. They were pure black, as if they were emptiness instead of substance. The sirening of crickets engulfed me. The crickets seemed before me, behind me, inside my head.

Though the air was getting cool, the porch felt warm against the back of my legs. I'd shaved them earlier, because my mother had changed the sheets that morning. Lately, I always shaved my legs when she changed the sheets. I liked the feel of smooth skin against fresh linen.

Someone knocked on the inside of the front door. I wasn't

sure what that meant. "Come in?" I asked. Ben came out and sat beside me on the porch.

"Is someone punishing you?" he said.

"No."

"Why did you tell Peter that man was the enemy? What did you mean? You made Peter cry."

"I wasn't trying to make anyone cry."

Ben gave me a dirty look, then scratched his crotch and burped. I considered drubbing him but saw he was about to cry himself.

Everyone came out, and we headed for the car. Charlie-O rubbed his hands through his thick hair. He smelled the way he always did when my brothers and I kissed him good-bye in the mornings and he'd just tamed his hair with Vitalis. He also smelled the way he sometimes did when he kissed us good night after he'd had a few Budweisers.

When we were driving to the party, he made a wrong turn almost as soon as we reached the next town. It was easy to do. The town was green. There was the wild green of sprawling oaks and maples, the honeysuckle vines in untended fields. Each street looked like the one before: green everywhere.

At the next corner, Charlie-O said, "Should I make a right here?"

"No," I said.

He turned anyway, too sharply, and we ended up in a ditch.

"Whoops, sweetie-dog," he said. "I thought you said yes. I thought she said yes."

We sat there for several minutes, as if we'd simply come to a very long traffic light. Eventually, Charlie-O said, "All right," and got out of the car, slipping almost immediately and falling to the ground. My mother and I got out to help him. He lay on the ground with his eyes open, blinking. We lifted him into the car, then patted down the dirt around the wheels. We weren't sure whether that was what we were supposed to do, but it made us feel better. I pushed in back with my brothers while our mother accelerated, the wheels whipping dirt into the air. The car didn't budge. Despite protests from my mother, my father got out of the car. "Aw, I can help," he said. He pushed with my brothers and me. I found myself pushing harder than before. My legs stretched out as I tried to get into a good position, and my cheek rested against the cool metal of the trunk. The effort took me over, and I realized how badly I wanted my father to be able to say later that he helped to get us out of that ditch. I thought that would help the marriage somehow. But it was no good. The car remained stuck. Finally my mother and I found a house, and a man came to help us. My mother took over the driving.

The novelist, whom Charlie-O played golf with sometimes, owned a small farm. The boy I liked was at the party, and he stood out back and talked with me while the grown-ups, mostly the fathers, got drunk. Some of the drunk men took off their blazers and dress shirts and got into a field and started chasing some animals—a few sheep, some pigs, and a goat. There was a dog, too. After a while a few of the women and some of the kids joined in. In fact, the man who owned the farm was running around with his wife and two kids. Everybody was chasing without actually trying to catch anything—they just felt like whooping and having fun. Some of the drunker men actually seemed to have taken on the personalities of the animals, for instance, one man began taking little steps, like the lamb he was chasing.

A couple of women were talking next to where the boy and I stood. They watched serenely, as if their husbands and friends were playing croquet or badminton.

"I adore that dress Marie is wearing," said one of them. Marie was the daughter of the novelist. She was having a great time running around.

"Isn't she getting married soon?" said the other woman.

"Yes."

"When is she getting married?"

"Oh," said the first woman, watching Marie fall on her face. "Some Saturday, I guess."

The boy frowned and bit his lip, as if he didn't understand

something, and then his face lit up with discovery. "Life is funny," he said.

I really liked that boy.

Charlie-O tackled the dog. "Got me a pig!" He looked at the animal in his arms. "Got me a dog," he said.

I chased the animals for a while. Once I caught a lamb in my arms, but instead of trying to get away, for a moment it just lay perfectly still. Then it kicked my shoulder, and we both yelped before it ran off. Across the field there was a tussle with the dog, and then everyone was up and chasing the animals again. I went to the sidelines to nurse my shoulder. Over the field, fleets of bleached clouds raced through the sky, and above the sounds of shouting rose the ubiquitous chirp of crickets.

Charlie-O, tired, walked over to me. His mouth was bleeding a bit—I guess from the struggle with the dog—but he was sweaty and happy, not happy with his life or with himself but happy with his exertion. He wiped his mouth. "Did you see that?" he said. "Thought I had me a pig."

The animals suddenly all spread out, running every which way, and there was general confusion in the field.

My father wasn't watching anymore. He had turned the other way and was gazing past me. I turned, too, and saw my mother coming forward. Charlie-O didn't move, but she walked over. They stood for an instant facing each other, and he gave her that look of his I saw sometimes—the one with the question in it. He seemed confused, then said, "Thought I had me a pig."

My mother was lovely and radiant, and suddenly she reached out to touch his face. The touch was sad, and also loving, sad because loving but not in love. "The boys are asleep," she said gently. "I think we'd better get going." She tugged at my hair affectionately and walked inside.

Charlie-O wiped his mouth again and turned to the field.

"Aren't we leaving?" I said. I wiped some mud off my face with my skirt.

He put his arm around the shoulder of the boy I liked,

who'd been standing with us. "So you like my daughter?" he said.

The boy's jaw dropped, almost imperceptibly, and then he sort of hunched up one shoulder and averted his eyes.

"She's a honey-dog, ain't she?" said Charlie-O.

"She is," the boy mumbled. He smiled with embarrassment, and he looked cute and silly. He had mud on his face, too.

Charlie-O put his other arm around me, and we stood and watched the end of the chase. A couple of people hoisted a pig into the air.

"Poor thing," said the boy. "I'm glad I ain't a pig."

Someone fell down, and the boy looked at me. "My dad!" he said. He hurried off to help.

"Are you okay, Dad?" I heard him say.

"Never felt better," said his father as he got up.

Charlie-O watched, not seeing. I looked down and saw a cricket hop onto his foot. "I never saw a cricket do that before," I said.

Charlie-O nodded abstractedly, and his face looked old in the same light that had made my mother so radiant. He still had his arm around me. "Promise me something," he said.

"Okay."

"Promise me you'll never break anyone's heart."

※※ 9

※※ My brothers, my mother, and I walked along the rim of the street. I pushed Peter along in the shopping cart we'd brought home the last time we'd all gone to the grocery. His scalp showed through his crew cut. My mother's throaty voice rose above the sound of the jangling cart. She was telling us a story I'd heard before. A long time ago, before my mother had got married, Obāsan came home one day with a powerful feeling of foreboding. She couldn't force herself out of the car. So she drove onto the lawn, right up to the house, until the door of the car sat two feet from the front porch. Then she got out and hurried inside. The next day, she found out a burglar had broken into a house five blocks south of hers at a quarter to six, and the police caught him trying to strangle someone five blocks north at a quarter after six. What my mother didn't add, but I knew from reading some diaries my grandmother left, was that she often had such fears. There were several times she drove onto a lawn like that. Still, I didn't think she was crazy. After all, in one case, fear may have saved her life.

I didn't say much when my mother finished talking. Lately, I hardly talked at all, except to yell. Nothing was too trivial for me to yell about. I was about to be famous in the family—among all my brothers and cousins, uncles and aunts, I would be the grouchiest. Already, when my brothers drew crayon pictures of me, it was with my mouth opened wide and frown lines on my forehead. Usually they colored my face blue.

My mother nudged me. "Oh, come on—you know that's a good story."

I nodded reluctantly. A single drop fell on my arm, and I started to run with the cart—Peter loved it. "Step on it!" I shouted. "It's raining."

We hurried along. The white daytime moon showed on a patch of turquoise sky between clouds. The rain was fine, like sifted flour. My mother was in a good mood but seemed aware this could easily pass. She looked at the rain and the sky as if they were possessions someone might take from her at any moment. The clouds suddenly seemed to be turning over themselves, and in a second they broke. We got drenched.

We spent nearly two hours in the grocery store. I was very particular about produce. I squinted at, smelled, shook, and tapped everything I bought. Once I looked up from the grapefruit and saw my mother speaking with Shane, her friend from Oregon, who hadn't left town yet. He was tall and angular, with bristly blue-black hair. He'd been born in Japan, and his real name was Tarō Nagasaki. I don't know where the Shane came from. Probably a movie or something. My mother seemed annoyed with him and started to walk off, pushing the cart. Ben and Walker trailed her. Shane followed, talking the whole time. Peter wasn't looking at them; he was looking at me, his jaw hanging open. My mother abruptly turned the cart around, and we finished shopping and left.

Outside, we walked down the street, and Shane followed, driving slowly along in his car while we ignored him. Finally my mother relented, and she and my brothers got in the car. I took the cart back alone.

When I got home, my mother and Shane were talking on the front porch. As I passed, Shane made a frightful noise in his throat and spit a couple of times up the walkway. I squirmed; I didn't understand men.

"Do your chores," said my mother as I went in.

My chores revolved around the kitchen: cooking rice; setting mousetraps; gathering garbage to burn in the incinerator; gathering flowers; defrosting the refrigerator. My idea of defrosting was taking a hammer and beating the ice senseless—it was my favorite household chore. "Yahhh! Take that!" I would yell as I hammered.

One time as I was working, I heard a friend of Ben's who was visiting ask nervously, "What's she doing?"

"She must be cleaning the kitchen," Ben said.

I always picked violets from a field nearby or cockscombs from the garden, and stuck the flowers any old place. That was the way we did things. Intricate lace curtains hung in all the windows, but none of the curtains matched, and baskets, statuettes, and pottery sat in every corner. Nothing matched, yet it all matched.

Rice and garbage chores were most important. We kept fifty-pound bags of rice in the garage—whenever we had visitors from out of state, they brought us rice. Every month or so, when the kitchen bag ran out, I went to the garage and dragged in a new bag. For breakfast we ate our rice in bowls with tea poured over it, or else on the side with brown eggs— eggs scrambled with shoyu and sugar.

That night we were going to eat outside, by the incinerator in the backyard. When the rice was cooked, I wet my hands in heavily salted water, shaped the rice into triangles for easy eating, and lined the triangles up on a tray. I took a couple of rice balls to my grandmother in the living room. From her snapshot, she gave me a critical look as I set down the rice, and I knew it was because I'd used too much salt for her taste. I started to walk away, but I turned back. "Okay, okay already," I said, and brushed off some of the salt.

In the kitchen I put the rice tray in the refrigerator and went to check the mousetraps. I used the stickum kind. I'd been lucky enough not to catch anything lately, but tonight I checked and found a cockroachy insect in one of the traps. It was so huge I was sure it was a mutant, and I thought about saving it as a gift for one of my brothers. But it started to struggle suddenly and seemed about to get away. I grabbed

the first thing I saw—a shoe of Charlie-O's sitting nearby—
and slammed it on the trap and picked the whole thing up.

"Olivia?"

Shane had come up behind me. I held the shoe out from
my body, my elbows straight, but he didn't seem to notice.

"You know, your mother's a stubborn woman," he said.

"Yes, sir," I said. He liked for us to say sir; I knew that
from Oregon. He thought we were barbarians and needed to
learn proper behavior. He would say things like: "If you
don't do the dishes you'll regret it someday," or "If you
don't clean up your room it will make your life a hell." I
thought I could feel the bug wiggling in the trap, but of
course it was my imagination. A syrupy fluid of indetermi-
nate color had started to seep out from under the shoe. "I'm
going to be sick," I said, but Shane still didn't notice anything.

"I'll bet she was spoiled and never got a good spanking."
He looked at me suspiciously. "When was the last time you
got a good spanking?"

"I'm way too old," I said, alarmed. "I have to go now. I
can talk later if you want." The bug juice was dripping over
an edge. I felt sweaty. Any second, the juice would touch
my skin. I stared at it, then at the finger Shane had just
pointed at my nose. I could feel my eyes crossing.

"Let me tell you a story," he said.

I stared at his finger, then at his face. "Lemme go!" I
said, as if he were holding on to me. My mother had started
the incinerator fire, and I charged out back. As I was running, I noticed it was actually one of Shane's shoes I was
holding. All of my parents' friends took off their shoes before
they entered a house. I threw Shane's shoe into the incinerator, with the trap attached. What else could I do? The shoe
didn't burn right away, but the laces did. I watched the glowing crisscrosses against the black shoe. When I turned, Shane
was standing at the back door with his hands on his hips.
"This better be good," he called out.

Sometimes friends dropped by while we did the garbage,
and if it was warm out, my mother gave everyone fruit-drink

ice cubes that melted quickly if eaten too near the fire, and colored paper fans that we used to get the fire going and to keep ourselves cool. Moths two and three inches across would flit back and forth over the incinerator before finally catching fire and collapsing into the flames. Sometimes if I'd caught a mouse in a trap, we'd throw it into the fire and watch the bulging eyes smoke and turn black. While Peter and Ben fought over who got to throw the mice in, Walker hid his eyes.

Now there was motion everywhere. Shadows from flames lunged across the grass. Diamond-shaped ashes flitted like moths above the fire; the sky seemed full of owls.

Shane came up behind me and stood silently for a moment. "Family and marriage," he said. "Inside family there's time. Outside, there's only decay."

At first I thought this was the start of the story he'd wanted to tell, but then I saw he was talking about his wife, who'd passed away years ago. I liked him for the first time; but mostly I wished he would go away. I was still tending the fire when I heard Shane's car pulling out of the driveway. I liked that sound.

When my father got home from work, we all sat on the front porch while the insecticide truck went up and down the streets, spraying the town as it did twice a week. Everyone in town always sat outside to watch, and the younger children used to run after the silvery spray as if chasing the brass ring. My mother was in a serene mood. I could tell my father sensed her serenity without looking at her. He knew her better than anyone else. That was his power over her, and, maybe, hers over him.

I decided to sleep that night on the small couch in the living room rather than in my bedroom. The front part of the living room, where the couch sat, was surrounded on three sides by windows, so there was a constant breeze. Sometimes I slept there because I wanted to feel separate from my normal life yet protected within it. It was like how when we first moved here I used to sneak out at night and wander in the small woods back of the house. The brilliant Arkansas night sky made me feel wild and displaced, like an animal child. Once, I managed to catch an owl in my hands. That's the way it was sometimes; we had a television inside, and a radio, but fires and birds and trees were what saturated my life and made it real. Yet even in the woods I felt safe, knowing my house was right there.

As I lay on the couch, I heard my parents talking at the living room entrance. "Is she asleep?" said my father. "I don't understand why she sleeps there." If they knew I was awake they would want me to get in bed. I lay still, imagining their worried faces. They worried about my brothers and me a great deal.

"Listen," said my mother. "She's not breathing evenly— she's awake." I made a snoring noise.

"No, she's snoring. She sounds just like Obāsan."

I stopped myself from saying, "I do not." No one spoke, and I thought they must be facing each other indecisively, talking with their eyes. Should they wake me? They walked away.

I sat up when my parents left. The hills made huge mounds in the distance. Ben's cat stretched on the windowsill, the curve of her back matching the curve of the black hills behind her.

A couple of friends came by later and said that another friend, Sally, was having a slumber party. I climbed through the window and out. In those days, when I was fourteen, I'd begun to have two lives: my life at home and my life with my friends. My family didn't know much about my friends, and my friends didn't know much about my family. I pictured a far-off future in which I spent all my time with friends and only visited with my family. It seemed hard to believe that would happen.

Sally lived in a huge gray frame house in the oldest part of town. Her house was a lot like mine, with a big basement and attic. Everyone was in the living room, speaking loudly to drown out the television no one was watching. "I'm not kidding," Liz was saying. "I'm not kidding." Liz had a deadpan voice and expression, and she always spoke with a note of finality. "The cutest guy was in the store the other day. When I laid eyes on him I told myself, Help me I'm drowning the world stops here I must meet that boy."

"Did you meet him?" Sally said.

"He left. My heart broke." Liz had a cigarette in her mouth and scissors in her hand—she was cutting another girl's hair. She waved the scissors for emphasis.

"And my heart broke. I was there, too," said Michelle. She was twelve. Her voice was the opposite of Liz's, squeaky and full of doubt. What was she eating now? It looked like cookie dough in her hand. Michelle's nightgown was just like the dresses her mother made her, except in flannel. Michelle wore nothing but her mother's creations—all jumpers from the same pattern but different material. Sometimes her jumpers had one pocket, sometimes two, and she owned one with three.

Sally was examining a scab on her elbow. "What was the worse moment of your life?" she said idly.

"Me?" said Michelle. "That's easy. It was at Dan's party last month, the first party anyone in my class had at night. Well, my mother is always getting me stuff that's really big, because she says I'm a growing girl. And she can't resist a sale. So the last time I needed underwear, she brought home ten pairs of the most gigantic underpants you've ever seen. They were size fourteen or something—*women's* sizes. I could take the elastic from the waist and pull it up to my chin.

"So at Dan's party I was kissing this boy Billy-Bob. He had his hands on my back. And, well, my underpants . . . All of a sudden I realized he could feel my underpants that were made for an elephant sticking out." She put her hand to her head as if she felt faint.

Sally said, "And yet he still liked you."

"It was awful." Michelle got up and ran to the couch, waving her arms in the air. She laid her head on the couch. "I'm crying, you guys," she announced.

Sally and I ran to see whether she was faking.

"You're not really crying," said Sally.

Michelle raised her head and pointed to a wet spot on the cushions.

"Saliva!" Sally and I said.

We watched TV, made phone calls, played cards, talked awhile, then got ready to go to a nearby lake. It was becoming light as we walked. Trina led the way. She was thin and pretty, with frizzy hair and a pointy nose and chin. She was fifteen, but I remember her seeming both young and old for her age. She and I had been good friends for a few months. She'd lived nearby, but I hardly saw her anymore. Her family was poor, even for Gibson. She'd had to drop out of school, and then, suddenly, it was as if she didn't matter in the same way to us any longer, because we assumed she was standing still while we were going forward. I don't think we assumed that consciously.

There weren't any cars on the streets, and most of the houses were dark. At the lake, we sat on a concrete ledge over the water. A wall rose behind us. I was so tired I could see sparkles and passing filmy clouds in the air. The water lapped on the side of the ledge below us. Someone had brought cards. The ledge wasn't quite wide enough for us to play in a circle, so we played sitting almost in a row.

Michelle dealt. "Hit me," said Sally. We started out saying "Hit me," and then as we got more tired we just said "Hit." Finally we weren't saying anything, just tapping our cards when we wanted another.

I quit and sat next to Louise and drifted off. When I woke up, Trina was leaning against the ledge. Her face looked even pointier than usual. The sky was a lovely green-blue. Michelle tried to shuffle the deck of cards, but half of them went flying over the water. Sally leaned forward and blinked several times at them as they spiraled down. "That used to be my father's lucky poker deck," she said. She shrugged and giggled, then flipped one of her slippers into the water. "My lucky slippers," she said.

"A button," said Trina, tearing one off and throwing it in.

"My favorite barrettes," I said. I threw in the rubber bands from my braids for good measure. I watched our trinkets fly into the lake.

It was a windless morning, and the water was barely lapping. Trina yawned extravagantly. "Does anyone have a watch?" she said, as if she had an appointment.

Louise stared sadly at the horizon. She stood up. "I'm going for a swim." She was a wonderful swimmer, but we were all very tired, and I didn't really believe she had the energy to go swimming now. Besides, she was wearing her nightgown, and the ledge was quite a way up. She jumped in anyway—she was always daring. We shouted at her.

"Lou, what are you doing?"

"You can't go swimming *now*."

Michelle said, "You'll get wet!"

We watched her a long time, but she didn't turn around. She got smaller and smaller and finally disappeared, fell off the earth—one second she was there, a shrinking dot, the next second she wasn't.

"A boat," said Trina. "We should get a boat." There were fishermen down the way. But I just watched what I couldn't see anymore. I admit a part of me hoped she wouldn't come back. She would swim to the other side of the lake and not return. She would be a legend in Gibson, Arkansas.

But we ran to the fishermen and told them to go after her. They listened mildly, as if it were the most natural thing in the world that a bunch of girls in their nightgowns should ask them to go chase their friend. They rowed after her. When they brought her back, they hardly talked to us. They got in the boat and rowed away. Louise was fine, just dripping and tired. In fact, everyone looked exhausted. Trina's skin looked oily and her hair scraggly. Liz was hunched over like an old woman. Michelle fell on her face, and no one even had the energy to tease her.

"What possessed you?" I said to Louise.

She said she couldn't remember anymore.

When I got home, the house was quiet. I passed my brothers' room and saw them sleeping. Walker always slept with his tongue hanging partway out. I got blankets from my room and went to sit on the couch in front. In a while I heard Walker yell, and I ran back. But he was still sleeping. I thought I saw things in his face I'd never seen before, sad things. I watched him until the sad things went away. It's funny how awful it feels to hear someone you love yell out, even if you know it's only from a dream.

When I returned, my mother was standing in the living room. She didn't look at me or say anything. I sat down and watched the hills, green now in the morning, blurry from morning mist.

My mother still didn't speak. She probably knew I'd sneaked out, and was getting ready to scold me.

"Where were you?" she finally asked.

"At the lake."

She pursed her lips and took a big breath but didn't let it out at first, as if it were caught inside her. Then she left. I wanted to talk to her. I wanted to tell her I was sorry if I'd added to her troubles. I wanted to ask her whether she had loved Shane and how much she had loved my real father, and whether she loved Charlie-O at all. I wanted to explain how when Louise had jumped, I was somehow there with her in the air, hanging halfway between the blue sky and the blue water, so that for a moment I couldn't tell whether we were rising or falling.

※※ Our assimilation into the community was easy enough. Most Japanese in Arkansas lived in Gibson or Lee, but there were a few others spread throughout the state. I got to know some of them at poker games during our first few years in Gibson.

At one time, nearly all Japanese in the area were men, plus a handful of women, who moved there to work in the hatcheries in Arkansas and Missouri. The women would already be married. The unmarried men later arranged marriages to women from Japan and raised families. Some chicken sexers spent hours on the phone each week, finding out what was going on in the business all over the country. When I lived in Gibson during the fifties and sixties, there were about five hundred sexers in the United States, most of them Japanese; today the younger ones are mostly Korean. The men who spent hours on the phone always knew where there were jobs, who got married and had kids, which hatcheries were thriving, which sexers worked for agencies and which were independent. If you lost your job in Arkansas, these men could tell you where to find another, usually in a small Midwestern or Southern town. People like my father were among the few Japanese who moved to these parts for reasons other than working for the hatcheries. We were bound to the Japanese in Arkansas just as my mother, father, brothers, and I were bound to each other; just as our relatives in

Los Angeles soon saw us bound to the residents of Gibson. So in this way my family was rooted in a community. I felt safe. That was the thing I liked most about Arkansas.

The grownups in the community had certain preoccupations. For the women it was us: the kids. For many of the men it was cards, and occasionally the horse races and the prostitutes in South Springs, in mid-Arkansas.

I grew up with cards. Solitaire and gin were perfect for the monotony of driving. Despite my small hands, when I was six I could make cards disappear behind the ears of my parents, or make the ace of spades always materialize at the top of the deck. When my brothers were old enough to play, each of us owned several decks, not including those with missing cards. My family had Bicycle decks, decks with tigers on the back, decks with wildflowers, and one deck my father got in the army that had naked ladies. He was very embarrassed when I found that deck one day while cleaning. "I never bought anything else like that in my life," he said, "but a man's got to be a man."

Sometimes on Fridays, if nothing else was doing, my father hosted a poker game. If the players were in a good mood, they let me deal a few practice blackjack or poker hands. In those days, gambling was legal in Arkansas, and I thought I might grow up to be a blackjack dealer in South Springs. My father, confounded by marriage, was becoming consumed with cards. I think this consuming involvement with cards marked something central to his life. The light left his eyes; he got old.

Yet I felt safe. I remember doing the garbage one Friday night while a game went on inside. I knew my father was gambling way too much. Yet still I felt safe. My brothers robotically threw paper piece by piece into the incinerator. The fire's heat distorted the air, so I watched my brothers through the bent air, as if I were viewing them through glass or water. They all had the same rounded cheeks, the same calm expression. My mother was roasting a hot dog over the fire.

There was an outburst of laughing and talking from inside.

She looked up. "Hurry," she said to me. "Go see who won that hand."

I was always running in and out of the house. My mother liked me to keep track of who was winning the poker game. She worried my father might be losing money. I got up and ran into the house. The players were taking a break. Charlie-O was fooling around, trying to amuse everyone by demonstrating how he could catch flying insects with the hose of our powerful vacuum cleaner. His best friend, who gambled infrequently, and mainly for social reasons, was laughing loudly. Everyone else smiled tolerantly, except for one man—Collie Asano—who looked at my father acidly. He lived just over the border, in Lee. He was older, in his late fifties, and had worked on a farm in California most of his life before the war. After that, he learned chicken sexing at a school, paid for by the G.I. Bill. His wife and kids had left him, and my mother said he owed thousands of dollars in gambling debts. I was scared my father would go into debt, too, or get like Collie. Collie had an air of being always fed up. Even when he told jokes he would seem fed up: with the joke, with everyone listening, with himself. I wondered whether he had ever been cheerful, like my father.

When I returned, my mother lifted her eyes from the fire. We'd been through this many times. Dull interest, like a flashlight whose battery is dying, brightened her face slightly.

"They're taking a break," I said, and the flashlight went out.

Life was placid that night. The early evening was full of thunder and lightning, though there was no rain. We ate watermelon for dessert, and the air filled with smells of fresh fruit and smoke. Peter fell asleep. When he woke, grumbling softly to himself, I took my brothers inside. I came out again and sat with my mother until I was sleepy, and then I returned inside. I don't know how late my mother sat up. Early the next morning, I looked out back from a window, saw the sun rising over the woods and the incinerator still smoking. I heard men's voices, so I went into the living room in my pajamas. The poker game was just breaking up. Collie was squinting at the ceiling. I looked up but saw nothing special. When I looked back down, he was glaring at me. I took a step back. "What are *you* looking at?" he said.

"I live here!" I said. But then I ran from the room.

The next night my mother went out, but I heard her telling my father that if he went gambling, he didn't have to come home that night. After she left, he told us he was going to Collie's and asked whether we wanted to come. It used to be that he always wanted to be with us, but in those days he always wanted to be with his poker friends. He went into the kitchen to make a sandwich, and my brothers and I took a vote—all four of us voted to go to Collie's. I knew that if we didn't go he would go without us, and I felt we were protecting him. Maybe we brought him good luck.

Collie lived down a long road with few other houses. As we turned down his road, I felt we were traveling to a different planet, a world that touched and even overlapped Gibson, yet remained somehow separate. The path to his house was surrounded by forests, with an occasional NO TRESPASSING sign tacked on a tree. I don't know whether there were animals or people watching from the trees, but I kept hearing rustling, and gunshots from deep in the bush. Hundreds of cicadas made moving patches on the road. The road itself seemed alive.

Before his poker binge, my father had smiled all the time. But as we walked he frowned without stop, and there was an urgency about the way he moved. Every so often a special look passed over his face, and I knew he was reliving a particular poker hand or dreaming about a future hand.

When we arrived at Collie's, the other players were waiting for my father. Collie's house was the opposite of mine. It was lean, almost spartan, full of geometry: angles, lines, squares. Pictures of his children hung on a wall, and on a doorjamb between a hall and the living room someone had made pencil marks measuring the growth of the children. I thought the pictures were still there because that was where his wife had left them, and he'd simply neglected to change anything from the way it had been. Neglect, I think, was a quality I associated with the world down Collie's road. Soon after we arrived, I dusted off the empty shelves in his house. It bothered me when they got dusty, as if the amount of dust coincided with some further deterioration of Collie's situation, and, by association, of my father's.

There were three other players besides my father and Collie. One of the only women who ever played was Toshi. She worked at a hatchery across the border in Missouri, with Collie and the father of the boy I liked, and she was slender and tough. Toshi always came out even. It was like magic; at the end of each night she had nearly the same amount of money she'd started with.

Vince Oh, a blackjack dealer from down south, came to games at Collie's only occasionally. He was young, in his twenties, and I thought there was something marvelous about him. He always concentrated intensely, yet he was the only one who ever smiled during play. Sometimes he flirted with me, but he flirted with Toshi, too, and once at a party I saw him flirting with my mother. He had beautiful long fingers.

The fifth person playing that night was William Kitano. According to my father, William was a "professional gambler," whatever that meant. When I'd first met him, a month earlier, he'd said, "A bill is something you get in the mail when you don't have any money; a will is something you write for when you die. Call me William, my love." Then he flicked my chin with his thumb. He was the opposite of Toshi—he either won big or lost big, usually won. There were strange rumors about him. People would say he could smell opposing players when they were bluffing, and could see their cards reflected in their eyes.

Everyone let me deal a few warm-up hands. I pretended I was in South Springs as I dealt. I pretended that my dealing was cool and precise, and that even the way my hair fell, the way my feet were planted, the way my shoulders leaned and swayed, were in harmony with my hands as they dealt. I tried not to let my face change, but I didn't want to seem blank, just precise, the way Vince had shown me he was when he worked. Because I was pretending to be elsewhere, it didn't seem like real money on the table. I really couldn't conceptualize Collie having lost thousands of dollars, nor could I quite imagine my father losing that much. That is, I could imagine it, but I couldn't imagine what would happen next, after he lost the money.

At Collie's that night, things got serious quickly. I dealt for only a minute before Collie lost his temper. "Get her out of here unless she's going to play," he screamed. Collie had oversized features—large ears and a large nose and mouth. He'd been nicknamed Collie because he wore his hair shaggy. His ears always got red as he screamed in his thin voice.

I took my brothers to play outside. The evening was warm and humid, and the sunset made the horizon look overlaid with red cellophane. A power plant made a huge complex pattern of dark lines against the sky, and my brothers seemed tiny by contrast. They spread out, playing some game.

After a while I looked toward the house. A fan was riffling the living room curtain. Everyone was taking a break. There were three windows in view—the living room, the kitchen, and a bedroom. Collie stood at one window, my father at another. They stared out, their faces shining, just barely, through the gauze curtains. Because the gauze washed out their features, they appeared oddly expressionless. I watched Vince and Toshi standing just outside the side door, talking, flirting, in a kind of dance. But they saw me and went in.

When everyone resumed playing, I kept running inside to check on things, the way my mother always had me do at our house. Every time I went inside, my father had less money. Finally I went in and he had no more money, yet he was still playing. He must have been betting money he didn't have. I went outside again. "Too rich for me," I heard Vince say, and then no one said anything. From the window I thought I could feel the heat from how hard they were concentrating inside.

Once, a couple of weeks earlier, everyone had considered letting me deal even during serious play, but Collie and William decided I might cheat for my father. Charlie-O got very angry with them and said I wouldn't cheat because I hadn't been raised to cheat. He was wrong in a couple of ways: I would do many things that were contrary to my upbringing, and though I was never tested, I thought I would have tried to cheat if my father were losing badly. I thought that again now. My family before my honor, I figured, not that I had so much honor to sacrifice.

I stuck my head in the window, only I couldn't find the place where the curtains separated, so I just batted and batted my hands around and mumbled "huh" and "what." When I finally got free and stuck my head through, the players were all looking at me as if I were a mirage. "Dad, we're tired," I said. "Wanna go home?" Collie's ears got so red I thought they would explode and fly off. I ducked down, and when I stood up again I saw through the gauze that everyone had returned to the game.

It was very dark, and when my brothers were tired we went into the kitchen. Earlier we'd put orange juice into an ice tray, and we took the tray out of the freezer. There were sixteen cubes, so we each got four. Ben devoured his quickly. "I'll trade someone their cubes for my Popsicle at home," he said. Peter and Ben negotiated.

"Shhh," Walker said. He cocked his head.

"It's Mom," I said. "What's she doing here?" We sat very still and listened to our mother's voice in the living room. She and my father were talking, not loudly, but with fire. The precious orange-juice cubes started to melt, but we didn't move. When my mother finally came in, she strode quickly to the table. The only thing she said was "I'm surprised at *you*." She said that to me.

"How did you know we were here?"

"Never mind."

"If we didn't come, he would have come without us. And we're good luck for him."

"Let's go. I brought the car." She left out the back door and we hurried after her, Ben slurping at an orange-juice cube he'd grabbed.

Our thongs squeaked to the car. The trees bending over the road made it seem as if a long cave lay before us. As we moved down the street we had to close the windows or the cicadas would jump into the car. Instead they hit the wind-shield like tiny demons and went skidding to the side. It was stifling in the car. The only noise was the motor and the tiny taps and thumps of the cicadas hitting the glass.

"Mom, I think he's really losing a lot," I said.

She pulled to the side and sat there for a minute before turning around and driving back to Collie's. We hurried across the grass to the house, but we stopped abruptly, sur-prised when we came upon Collie standing outside. He was urinating, high against the front door. He turned to look at us, then splashed a quick sideways figure eight on the door before zipping up his pants. "See my house?" he said. "It's an illusion. It's not really there."

I looked at the house. Surrounded by dark and trees and below an orange-ringed moon, it did seem not quite real. That's what I thought he meant.

"Now leave me alone. I'm thinking."

My brothers and I stood there until our mother pulled us inside. Our father had fallen asleep on the couch, and Ben ran and jumped on him. "Did you lose? Why are you sleep-ing?"

"Huh? What are you doing back?"

Toshi was cleaning off the table, emptying ashtrays into each other. Vince sat at the table, idly shuffling. William stood with his back almost flat against a wall, looking every-one over as if studying for a test. I felt weird standing in this house that wasn't real.

"*Did* you lose a lot?" said my mother.

Charlie-O paused. "No, it got too rich for me, so I dropped out, and then, I don't know, I guess I fell asleep." My mother didn't answer, and I could tell she wasn't sure whether he was lying. I thought he was tell-ing the truth. I thought he had dropped out, but almost had not. Relief washed over my mother's face—she must have decided he wasn't lying. She'd probably decided that for the same reason I had. The alternative was deciding he was lying and had lost a lot. Peter climbed onto his

shoulders and we all went out of the house. My father
set Peter down on top of the trunk. Ben yelled out, ''I
have to go to the bathroom,'' and ran back inside, Walker
following. Ben was calling Walker a dummy for thinking
our father had lost, and Walker was calling Ben a dummy
for the same reason. Collie stood with his hands on his
hips.

''Which one of them can do imitations?'' he said.

''The middle one,'' I said. ''Walker. He can do Ed Sullivan so well it's amazing.''

''Everyone can do Ed Sullivan.''

''He can do anything. He can do our pet dog. He learned
how to bark before he could say 'dada.' He can imitate things
that aren't even alive, like a flag in the wind or a bouncing
ball.''

Collie nodded, kept nodding long after anything had been
said. ''That would be great. That would just be great.''

''Which? To know how to bark?''

''To be able to imitate anyone you wanted.''

''How come?''

''Then you'd never have to be yourself.''

Peter slid down from the car. He stared at Collie. Collie's
face was twitching, as if an invisible hand were pressing at
it. Peter put his hand in mine, and we waited while my father
took Collie aside to talk briefly. When Walker and Ben returned, we all got in the car. As my father started the ignition, I looked back and saw Collie standing watching. Then
I looked at Peter watching Collie. Collie could probably just
make out the presence of faces in our window.

''I feel scared,'' Peter said. He kept watching Collie, and
Collie kept watching us. He looked much the way Peter did,
scared, as if he could not quite understand what he was seeing. That's when I realized that by calling his house an illusion, he meant that because of his gambling debts, pretty
soon his house would no longer belong to him. Maybe it did
not belong to him at this moment. The funny thing was how
after Collie faded, I could still see his house, as if he himself
were the illusion.

* * *

A year and a half later, I got a job inoculating chickens at the hatchery Collie had worked at, but he wasn't there anymore. He had lost his house and moved on. I never saw him again.

✳✳ *11*

✳✳ The highway spreads itself through quiet, humid land, curling with two lanes through the Ozarks, and later opening to four lanes and passing through the centers of towns—it was the main street of Lee, Fort Jefferson, Hilldale, Ashland, and countless other places.

One summer in Hilldale, I found a forbidden family. This was when we'd first moved to Arkansas. The family lived in a house you weren't supposed to walk by alone. Curious, I rode my bicycle past one day and was so busy trying to see into the house I didn't see a branch on the sidewalk. The family, the Masons, bandaged my leg with toilet paper and masking tape, and I sat with them on their porch for supper every day for months afterward.

The Masons had lived in six different cities—Philadelphia, New York, Washington, Boston, Newark, and Baltimore. I had lived in none. The first night I ate with them, a pointy-faced girl a little older than I sat next to a pile of fashion magazines she was intently leafing through. Some of the magazines were quite old, but a couple were newer. At the rate she was going, it would take several hours to get through the pile, but she was going at it with admirable determination. I'd never looked through a fashion magazine, but she shared.

The family was a mother, five kids, and the mother's boyfriend. I think the main reason parents warned their kids away was because the mother and the boyfriend were living together.

We used to eat chili right out of the can for supper, and sometimes we had Campbell's soup cold out of the can—mushroom was my favorite.

"The night of my wedding right before we had sex," the mother, Ugly Sarah, said one night during supper, "I thought, Is this going to hurt? And then, during sex, I thought, Is this sex? When it was all over, my husband said, 'Are you alive?' " She took hold of my nose and turned my face back and forth. "Honey, that was a *long* time ago." I giggled. Sarah's face under the porch light was plump, almost doughy. She was okay-looking, but Ugly Sarah was how she introduced herself, and it was what a lot of people called her.

She said her husband's last words the day he walked out, when she was twenty-eight, were "Your tits have sagged two inches in two years." At times I loved her so much I wished I could offer her my youth, though I doubt she would have wanted it.

When she said that about her husband leaving, the daughter who always had fashion magazines looked up. "I don't remember him at all," she said, then looked back down. The girl was named Trina. Later Sarah and her boyfriend got married, and the whole family moved to Gibson, where my parents reluctantly allowed me to be their friend.

Lucy Asano was born in Lee and lived there until she was thirteen. I ran into her once when we were both visiting Arkansas in our mid-twenties. She said she felt no bursts of nostalgia, no sadness and no happiness, to return.

She used to boast how her father had sexed more chickens in his life than the city of New York could eat in a year. She said he could sex thirteen hundred an hour, best in Arkansas.

One thousand was considered very good, eight hundred good, six hundred acceptable if you were accurate. Fewer than that, it wasn't worth anyone's time. She wasn't like the children who ignored their fathers' Japanese friends in public, especially the friends who worked as sexers.

Lucy never knew what days or hours her father, Collie, would be home. When he wasn't working, he was often gambling. His life was breaking then. Even years later, when he spoke of Lee, his voice was always bitter.

At night, when her father was out gambling, Lucy would lie in bed awake, her thoughts like a net, catching the sounds of rain on the roof, her sister breathing, the cat scratching the couch on the other side of the house, and finally the sound she was waiting for, her father slipping through the front door. Sometimes he fell asleep on the living room couch, too exhausted to make it to her parents' bedroom. Once, she sneaked into the living room and saw her mother slapping her father on both cheeks and crying silently, so as not to wake the kids. Another time, she sneaked into the living room and they were sleeping naked on the couch.

A week later, her mother took Lucy and the kids away.

It was the holiday custom in Gibson for each family to line its curb with lighted candles in translucent wax bags on Christmas Eve. One year, my mother let me have Trina and Lucy stay overnight. We all lighted candles in winds that jostled the bags but left the flames intact. I got faint burns on my hands, but my hands were so cold I thought the burns were some sort of frostbite. Down the street, the flames in front of the neighbors' houses stretched into the distance, the spaces between them getting smaller and smaller until they blurred into a line of lights. The lights were supposed to lead Santa Claus to each house in turn. My family had never believed in Santa Claus, but you couldn't help believing in something as you watched the flames. My father was telling my mother about a "fancy investment" some people in town had lost money on. I stared down the road of lights, imagining the view of Gibson from the hills. Trina, Lucy, and I shivered silently before going in to bake with my mother. We were the best of friends, but by the next Christmas Trina had dropped out of school and Lucy was gone.

12

※※ Getting a job at the hatchery, when I was sixteen, shifted the focus of my life from my family to work and the boy I liked. When I wanted to know about work, I asked my father. When I wanted to know about love, I asked my mother. But when I wanted to know about sex, I asked my grandmother. This was difficult, of course, since she had already punched the clock. That may not sound like a very respectful way to talk, and as you know I didn't like my grandmother much when she was alive, but "punched the clock" was one of the phrases she always used to talk about people who'd died, and I think she would have preferred me to be unsentimental about her death. My grandmother was a realist.

I got her opinion through her diaries, small parts of which were in Japanese. Translating them was difficult—my mother did all the hard parts, and some parts she refused to translate at all. But the project was well worth my time. It was good for me to have someone to consult with, because sometimes I needed to straighten things out in my mind. And I liked the two languages, Japanese and English, how each contained thoughts you couldn't express exactly in the other. For instance, because you didn't use spaces between words in the same way in English and Japanese, certain phrases—such as "pure white" or "eight slender objects" or "how many people"—seemed to me like only one word in Japanese. Seeming to use only one word changed slightly the meaning of what I was saying. It made me think about what exactly was pure white and not merely white.

The boy I liked was named David Tanizaki—Tan. He had grown up in Georgia and spoke with a heavy Southern accent. He said things like "Hot dawg" and "Gawd damn," and he was enthusiastic about everything. His father got quite friendly with mine, and Tan and his family used to come over for supper all the time. Mr. Tanizaki was a fabulous dancer, and he and his wife and my parents often danced for an hour or two after they ate. Later Mr. Tanizaki and my father would dance, a wild running-around-the-room war dance to a wild war dance record that Mr. Tanizaki had acquired on a trip to New York or Newark or Buffalo, someplace like that. Tan's father was an intense man, with a frenetic energy I sometimes felt he controlled only with his fervent belief in discipline. It was as if half his energy were turned inward, controlling the other half. He hardly ever smiled, even when he was having fun, yet watching him jumping and dancing, I knew he was happy. That's sort of how Tan was, too, except less intense and less disciplined. Both of them had the same gold skin and gold arms and legs, but Mr. Tanizaki's hair was white and Tan's was black.

Tan and I both worked at the hatchery in Missouri where his father and Toshi worked. Tan did general labor—hauling barrels, washing incubators—and I inoculated chickens, with a group of several other women. Actually, everyone called us "the girls," though some of the inoculators were in their fifties and sixties.

My parents didn't really want me to work at the hatchery. They thought it would be too hard and awful for me, and might make me cynical. And though at first I worked just on weekends, it *was* awful when I started. I was supposed to stick the vaccination needles into the necks of newborn chicks, and a couple of times I broke a neck by accident. But I wanted to work there. I thought it would prove I could do work I hated, in case I should ever have to, to survive. I planned to work full time during the summer, to prove to myself I could. The hatchery paid me, in cash, what I thought was a great deal of money. Tan also got paid cash. He was sixteen, like me, but he'd started working there when he was fourteen.

I liked to be around Tan. Sometimes during breaks we would go to an abandoned bus sitting on the grass near the hatchery and make out, laying a blanket on the rusted floor. We thought it was very daring to take off our shoes and socks and shirts, there where we so easily might be discovered. So I liked that aspect of working at the hatchery.

Another reason I liked the job was that the sexers were mysterious to me: I liked to watch them. Someone had told me they separated the chickens not by picking them up and looking at them but by instinct, picking them up and instinctively "feeling." I later found out that wasn't true. One of the sexers had told this to a white reporter, and the reporter believed him, so now some people thought it was true. Sexers worked long hours, but a few of the younger ones, at this hatchery and others, managed to buy Cadillacs. I think my parents disapproved of Cadillacs—too ostentatious. Once in a while some of the younger workers rented a private plane and flew down to South Springs to play poker. Once, a nisei girl sang at a nightclub there, and all of us drove down to see. It was like a field trip for me. The nightclub let me in even though I was underage, because I said I was the girl's cousin. She was sort of a corny singer, but we all felt very proud of her and thought she might go far.

None of the sexers ever came to work late, and none of them at the hatchery where I worked had missed a day for the past year. Toshi hadn't missed a day in five years, and some years she didn't get a vacation. These people seemed unreal to me. One of them told me he hated the work so much when he started that he often felt he was being choked— he literally felt hands around his neck. That man hadn't missed a day in three years, someone told me. I couldn't believe how tough and tense they all were. Yet I liked them, and I wanted them to like me.

My workroom was separate from theirs, but I could see them through the wide doorway. Sometimes Tan would go into their room to help clear away the barrels of male chicks that someone would drown out back later. The hatchery dealt with layers so you didn't need the males. The hatchery was a noisy, ugly place, but because I was sixteen and this was all new to me, and because the place felt so real—so *close*—it possessed a sort of mean sexuality. Though I'd not yet slept with Tan and though I worked only once or twice a week, I thought about him and the hatchery all the time: I could be obsessive like my mother. I felt as if I were a pendulum between Tan and work, but I didn't feel I was swinging on my own so much as I was allowing myself to be pulled back and forth between the two.

It was while we were talking in the bus that Tan and I first decided to sleep together, but we made the final arrangements at his house in Lee—less mean there, less ugly. We discussed things alone in his room. I suppose we just could have done it then and there, but we chose a date a few weeks in the future. Later, as we walked from his house to mine, it was hard to talk in any intelligent way with so much else on our minds; plus, I kept thinking about my grandmothers diaries: I wanted advice.

We walked a foot or so apart in the road, sort of shyly, very aware every time we happened to touch. Everything around us seemed very sexual to me: the slope of the hills, the way the humid Arkansas air felt just slightly heavy. Even the way we weren't touching created a sort of dizzying tension.

When we got to my home, my mother was standing outside, chatting with a friend. They were talking about Mr. and Mrs. Oyama, who lived a few towns over. Apparently he'd had his stomach removed; afterward, he put the stomach in a jar on the mantelpiece, to remind his wife and family what a hard life he'd had. "Doesn't his wife mind?" said my mother.

"Oh, yes, but that's just because she's jealous. She thinks she's had a hard life, too, but she doesn't have a stomach in a jar to prove it." We all laughed, and my mother's friend turned amiably to Tan. "How are your parents?" she said.

Tan never really hid his feelings. Now his face fell. His father was having problems at work lately, though I wasn't sure what kind of problems.

Tan just said, "They're fine," kissed me good-bye, and left, and I could tell he would go off and sit somewhere in a bad mood now.

I went inside and heard my mother and her friend lower their voices and giggle—talking about me and Tan, no doubt, and how "cute" we were. My parents were always talking about and watching me lately. Occasionally I thought they said things just to see my reaction. In a couple of years I was going to be sent into the real world, like America's first spaceship. My parents expected there to be some glitches, but they would get better at this each time: after me would come my brothers. Once, my mother started crying suddenly, and I knew it was over something from a long time ago. Nobody said anything, but everyone looked pointedly at me. The looks meant it was my obligation to leave Arkansas someday and have a happier life than my parents had. I think they wanted me not only to hate working at a place like a hatchery but also to hate the hatchery itself, as if I couldn't leave the world it represented without also, at some level, disdaining it.

While my mother and her friend continued laughing and talking, I sat in the living room, in front of the shrine we'd made for my grandmother. The shrine had been fairly traditional at first, with just Obāsan's picture, the shot glass of water, and the bowl of rice. In the cabinet the water and rice sat on, we kept a couple of my grandmother's things: her diaries and the long braid my mother had cut off when she'd died—my brothers and I had reunited the strands. The cabinet was so humid inside that some of the diary pages started to change and warp, as if they were alive, growing.

After a time, we'd begun to hang other pictures on the wall behind the cabinet. First we taped up a picture of my grandmother as a young woman, then a picture of her with my brothers and me; then one day someone put up a picture of my brothers and me alone, at a farm somewhere in California. Finally, though a snapshot of my grandmother was still in the center, we now had pictures of whatever appealed to us: a house in Hawaii someone had seen in a magazine; an advertisement for Coca-Cola; a baseball player; a dog we used to own.

My grandmother's diaries were a revelation to me. Besides her three husbands, she'd had seven lovers—unusual for her day. Her first great lover was not someone she'd married. Before she ever slept with him, she wrote: "I like the diabolical quality, the clarity of admitting I *want*, knowing he knows, and now waiting to see it happen, or not happen." The first time I read that, I was stunned, that such wanting could have a "diabolical" quality. I became enamored of the very word. That man, who could inspire diabolical wanting, was the only one of her lovers I cared to read about just then. Later she wrote more about him: "He still had all his clothes on and I was undressed when we started to argue, yet I didn't feel vulnerable. I felt strong." That's what I wanted, to feel the same strength, more than I wanted love.

Tan and I always took the same route to meet each other. We'd call each other, talk for a minute, hang up the phone, then leave our houses and meet somewhere in the middle. The night we first slept together, it was very hot out, and I'd been taking showers all day so I would smell fresh. I had never been so clean. My whole skin ached with cleanliness.

Both Gibson and Lee had an unplanned quality. It was as if a giant had taken a bunch of houses and thrown them randomly on the ground, and people took up residence wherever the houses happened to land. Most people lived in frame houses or mobile homes, but residences ranged from rich Mr. Baldwin's two-story brick house to several unfinished-wood houses without plumbing or heating; migrant farm families lived in those houses. Tan's place, like mine, was in between.

His bed was small and uncomfortable. It lay at a slant, and he said he always woke up with his face pressed against the wall. We had planned to use his parents' bed. You would think we would feel very adult about all this, but instead we felt childlike—sneaky and excited.

We made out for a long time under the covers. Kissing was my favorite thing in the world. Sometimes when we kissed under the covers, it got very hot. This created the illusion there was no air around us but we were sort of kissing air into each other.

Finally it got too hot underneath, so we took off the covers and started to get completely undressed. I felt panicked. "What about the sheets? We should do this on the bathroom floor."

"No, I've got a towel—here."

"No, no, that's not good enough. We have to use the bathroom floor."

He took a deep breath but said okay. We ran half dressed into the bathroom and I lay down. The tile was cool against my back. We got completely undressed and kissed some more. But the floor seemed cold and hard, and when I opened my eyes, the light from outside seemed to accentuate the hardness. "Oh, this is no good," I said. "We have to get back in bed."

"Let's just stay," he said, breathing hard.

"Well, okay." I closed my eyes as tightly as I could. "I'm ready," I said, bravely. When nothing happened, I opened my eyes.

He looked at me as if he had amnesia. Then he looked surprised, then frustrated. "Okay okay," he said, half pulling me up. We stood and I saw his erection and was so surprised I walked into the doorjamb on the way out. When we got in bed I was surprised how ready I was, and how easily he slipped in. He moved in and out hard at first, making my head hit against the headboard. I wouldn't have minded, except I was scared I might get knocked out, and then I'd miss the most important part; but that didn't happen.

I expected that afterward I would feel some emotion related to love, and I did, but I also had a peculiar feeling a shade shy of self-confidence.

I wanted to lie awhile, but we had his family to think

about. They might be returning soon. Tan seemed confident, shy, and sheepish all at once. He turned to look at me. "Wanna sandwich or something?" he said; I thought he was sweet.

We got dressed and made the bed, and then, as if starving, we cleaned out his refrigerator. We ate two three-layer sandwiches apiece, five oranges between us, a pot of tomato soup, and a half gallon of milk. We were washing dishes when his parents, sisters, and brothers got home. We all talked about the hatchery for a few minutes, then Tan took me outside. The roads and fields were covered again with patches of cicadas, and the air was filled with what sounded like one, unified cry. When my grandmother was my age, she'd written, she used to catch cicadas and crickets and put them into small cages in her room, so she could listen to them sing; also, she thought they brought her good luck.

When we got to my house, my mother and the same friend who'd been over a few weeks earlier were chatting in the same place as before, as if they'd been standing there talking all that time. It seemed Mrs. Oyama had decided she had stomach problems, although she couldn't find a doctor to corroborate it.

Tan and I stood on the front porch to say good-bye. "Ooh, they're saying good-bye," said my mother's friend quietly, but not too quietly. Tan smiled a private smile at me. But he had to get up earlier than I did for work the next day, and his face already carried that weight. My confidence dissolved, but my love stayed the same. Tan walked off. The cicadas on the asphalt made a path, so there was a constant flurry about him, like electrons around a nucleus as he returned home to his life, which was separate, now, from mine.

When summer started, I began full time at the hatchery. Tan and his father often picked me up for work. I lived out of their way, but I think Tan talked his father into coming for me. They were very close. A lot of kids my age were sometimes embarrassed by their parents. But Tan never felt that way.

When there was time, his father liked to show off for my family. Mr. Tanizaki was the highest jumper I knew; also the fanciest. We used to hold a yardstick next to him, and he would shoot straight up, past the top of the stick. He could also spin around twice without touching the ground, or click his heels twice to the side as he jumped. He could balance a book, or a basket, or, if we begged him, even a clothes hamper, on his head as he did his double turn. We all thought this was quite impressive, especially the hamper.

Sometimes Tan, my father, my brothers, and I joined Mr. Tanizaki, everyone trying to outdo everyone else. When I was in a grown-up mood, I didn't participate; all this jumping seemed to me an undignified affair. Besides, I didn't like to do anything if I couldn't be best. And Mr. Tanizaki was always best. He shot skyward, off an invisible trampoline, while my brothers, ordinarily graceful, appeared to plod and trip around him.

I think Mr. Tanizaki liked to jump around so he could work off some energy and be calm enough for his job. He was usually feeling more restrained by the time we reached the hatchery. He always waited a moment before going inside. He would take a big breath, almost as if he were about to jump into a pool, before he went through the door.

The hatchery was an ugly building in one of the most beautiful parts of Missouri. There were only a couple of farmhouses around, one in the distance, and one, across the highway, that sometimes had rolls of hay drying in the fields. A great many trucks passed by, no matter what time it was, sometimes two or three trucks in a row—produce trucks, livestock trucks, more produce trucks. The hatchery sat back from the highway, fronted by tall maples. It was concrete, windowless, and I imagine no one who passed took notice of it. Because the building had no windows, on warm days it seemed to exist in a cavern of heat and moisture.

Everyone was supposed to go through a back door rather than the reception area, which was always empty. There was a pan of soapy water by each of the doors; you were never to enter the building until you cleaned the bottoms of your shoes, to minimize the chance of spreading germs in the building. The owner didn't always clean off his shoes, but the workers did. It was just that none of us wanted to get blamed if something happened to the newborn chicks.

Sometimes the sexers, Tan, and I stayed overnight at the hatchery. The sexers worked seventeen hours, slept five, worked seventeen. My hours were not so bad, so I got more sleep. All the sexers had jobs at other hatcheries, and they often worked as long as thirty or forty hours in a row at their various hatcheries. They took Dexedrine to stay awake and to help them drive from one hatchery to another. When I stayed over, I brought a flowered overnight bag, a sleeping bag, and a paper sack with my meals, including plates and flatware. The sexers, even the toughest and most jaded of them, couldn't help smiling the first time I dragged in my gear.

Toward the middle of summer, there was a great deal of tension focused around Mr. Tanizaki at the hatchery. Sexers were hired not as individuals but as groups: the management hired and fired groups, not individuals, while the group hired and fired the individuals. Of course, the members of each group changed over time. Since Collie had left, Mr. Tanizaki had been in his group the longest—twenty years. Altogether he'd worked sexing chickens for thirty years, and he said that sometimes at night he woke up and found himself moving his hands, quickly and expertly, in the motions he used for work.

Unless you were with an agency, every group had a leader, who negotiated with the management in return for a commission from the rest of the workers. When one person did bad work, that put everyone's job in jeopardy. The manager at Mr. Tanizaki's hatchery had spoken to the group's leader and said their work was marginal lately. The manager kept careful records on the group's performance, and if even one person did bad work, it showed up in the statistics. I'd never seen Mr. Tanizaki having problems at work, but I'd heard rumors about him. The rumors varied: he was taking too much Dexedrine; he was losing his mind; he was getting lazy. I didn't think it was any of those things, or maybe it was all of them. He just seemed tired. Still, everyone was tired, and I didn't know why the others thought he might be doing bad work—sometimes it bordered on the supernatural how they knew things about each other.

The manager complained a second time. When I heard, I could almost see lines being drawn, loyalties to the group solidifying. One more complaint and I knew Mr. Tanizaki would probably have to quit, which was preferable, or be fired.

During work one day, Tan and I stood drinking coffee and watching Tan's father prepare his hands. Though he wore gloves as he worked, he carefully washed his hands before and after his shifts and during each break. He stood at the sink washing each finger, even under his nails, and then he put on moisturizer. He didn't groom himself particularly well—his wife cut his hair unevenly, and his clothes didn't always match—but, as if in defiance of his job, he kept his hands immaculate, like the hands in a watch or a ring advertisement.

Eight sexers worked at the hatchery. Two of them were telling jokes about a prostitute they both know, and I could see that Toshi, the only woman sexer, was on the verge of telling me to the leave the room, not because she thought I was too young to hear but because, I think, I was something of an outsider. I had a feeling that my outsideness affected the pattern of things, and perhaps one reason I never witnessed Mr. Tanizaki's problems at the hatchery was because Toshi and the others somehow subtly and instinctively hid them from me. Next to my parents and the Tanizakis, Toshi was the adult I liked most in Arkansas. She had an amazing face, one that seemed to change from distrust to apathy from moment to moment, like one color to another and back again in the space of three seconds.

All of a sudden one of the men was yelling at Tan's father. "You haven't got the balls," he said. When he said "balls," he brought his hands down to his crotch and gave one quick jerk. The man blocked the way between Mr. Tanizaki and the sink.

Mr. Tanizaki raised his eyes slowly. Toshi took a drag from her cigarette as if she hadn't heard a thing, then she turned to Tan and me. "Get out," she said.

I wasn't going to leave unless Tan did. His eyes met his father's, and I don't know what he saw there, but he took my hand and we left.

It was raining hard, so we stood in a doorway. There was a large light outside the hatchery, the beam spotlighting the rain so that the lamp resembled a giant showerhead. Tan and I ran across the wet grass to the abandoned school bus sitting in the field. Most of the seats were ripped, with stuffing hanging out, and most of the windows were broken. I touched my cheek against cracked glass, then sat up and touched my other cheek against Tan's face. I was surprised by the way his face felt cooler than the glass. I could smell the rain, sweet and clean. The fresh beauty around us was almost confusing. It was right there, I could see it, yet it seemed far away, someplace else. Sometime in the last few weeks, I'd stopped feeling challenged by the idea of having what I now saw as an onerous job. Lately, I felt mildly irritated a lot, but now I felt a sort of scared sadness.

"I slept out here once with a friend a few years ago," said Tan.

"In the bus? That sounds fun."

"Not really. It wasn't even a friend, just some kid a lot of other kids in his neighborhood didn't like. He'd got beat up a few times, but his father didn't care. One night he came over to my house, real scared. My parents had company, so he couldn't stay, but I told them I was going to his house, and we came here."

"Did he ever stop getting beat up?"

Tan shook his head no. On the highway, the rain hit the pavement and bounced off, sweeping upward like dust. Rain pounded on the bus top. "In fact, he got his nose broke once and ran away. Then his family moved. He probably ran away some more. I don't know." Tan spoke tiredly.

"Why do you think of that now?" I said. He didn't answer. I shivered. It was warm, but I felt cold. Tan had a
funny expression on his face. I thought how if he'd had the
same expression ten years earlier, as a little boy, it would
mean he was about to cry. But of course ten years earlier he
could have cried. Now we sat staring quietly out the front
windshield, as if the bus were moving. Finally I had to go
inside. Tan didn't have to get back to work yet. I left him
sitting, a bit stiffly, staring out the front window.

The other vaccinators had already started. I took my place
next to the woman in charge. Officially the hatchery manager
was my boss, but this woman had taken over the inoculators,
as if we were an army within an army, and I always got my
orders from her. But I had trouble liking her; she was the
most adept worker, and sometimes she made disparaging
remarks to the rest of us. Sometimes as I inoculated, un-
pleasant feelings would rise in me, feelings of hate and
toughness toward my work, and I would hate her, too.

Tonight I was in a competitive mood. I almost enjoyed
myself. I liked the feel of my hands moving efficiently, when
a few months before they had been clumsy. I started a contest. Every time the woman in charge picked up a chick and
shot it with her needle, I tried to shoot one, as well. But after
a few minutes I was already way behind. Pretty soon I could
taste salt on my upper lip, and the noise of the chirping
seemed to be getting louder. I began to feel tired and paranoid, and I thought the woman in charge was somehow responsible for making the noise increase.

In a little while, I became aware that I was the only one
still working. The other girls were unmoving, watching the
sexers in the huge room next to ours.

Inside their room, the only light came from metal lamps
dangling over each worker's table. Crates of newborn chicks
rose in piles throughout the room, a maze of crates. The only
sounds were the chirping and the radio. But they were so
constant they didn't seem like noise anymore. Everyone was
staring at Mr. Tanizaki. He stood up to get another box of
chicks to work on. I could see nothing wrong. Then the

others returned to their jobs. While Mr. Tanizaki worked, his shoulders swayed as if to a music derived from the work itself. The radio played something languid, but I thought he was unconscious of it. He *was* his work: you couldn't separate which was the man and which the work.

Toshi appeared fastest. She moved her hands fluidly and economically rather than with the large rounded movements some of the others used. Each of the sexers could sense what the rest were doing; if one stood, or even just yawned, the others seemed to know. Once Toshi stretched her back, and a man, without looking up, said, "Getting tired, Toshi?" I picked up my needle, but in a few minutes I sensed—I don't know how—that everyone else had stopped again.

"Me and my wife are thinking of getting a new car," announced Mr. Tanizaki. The others looked at him as if they had no opinions, had never had any opinions, and never would have any opinions. "I want to get a Chevy, but my wife says Ford."

Nobody watched him now except me. Everyone else had turned back to work, as if on some secret signal. Mr. Tanizaki tapped Toshi on her back. "Don't you have a Chevy?" he said.

She worked for a couple more seconds, then lifted her eyes to him. "I beg your pardon?" she said. Everyone was watching again.

"Do you have a Chevy?"

She opened her mouth to speak, thought better of it, closed her mouth, opened it, then closed it, and lowered her eyes to her work.

Mr. Tanizaki wasn't fazed. "Furthermore, me and my wife can't decide between a blue car or a red one. What time is it, anyway? When did we have our break?"

Toshi looked up and caught the eye of Nori, the man who'd had words with Mr. Tanizaki earlier. Mr. Tanizaki was speaking to the wall. "I don't know, you live without a car, and then everyone else gets one and you feel like you have to get one, too. But when you think about it, what do you need a new car for? And does it matter what color it is?"

Nori scooted out of his seat and left the room. Several others followed. Mr. Tanizaki still talked. I tried using ESP to make him quiet down. "It's keeping up with the Joneses, that's all it is," he was saying. "But I ask you, what's so bad about that? Why not keep up with them?"

The remaining sexers left the room without speaking. A couple of them accidentally bumped the lamps over their tables, and the swinging lights made the shadows move, made it seem the whole stale room were shaking. I felt dizzy. The inoculators left, and I went over to Mr. Tanizaki.

"Do you have a new car?" he said.

He knew we didn't. I glanced behind myself and around the room, but everyone had gone. I felt at a loss. I started to tell him the first thing I thought of, how Charlie-O was trying to sell a car he'd fixed up just like new. This was as good a time as any to try to make a sale. "Want to buy a car?" I said; maybe my father would give me a commission. But then sanity happened to return, and I said, "You need to go for a walk. It's stuffy in here."

"Is it?" he said. He turned back to his table, and when I tried to talk more, he didn't reply. He just kept mumbling to himself.

"Don't go anywhere," I said to his back. "I'll get Tan."

A few people were smoking in the hall, but Tan wasn't among them, so I left. Outside, the fireflies were sprinkled over the fields, as far as I could see. In the distance, an owl swooped and rose again.

Toshi and a couple of others were standing by a tree. "Yeah, it's cutthroat," she was saying. "It wasn't so bad a few years ago; nobody was always trying to steal your territory."

"I heard National Chick Sexing wants this hatchery," said a man.

"We could lose our jobs."

"We should just fire him. He won't change. People never change. They just get worse."

"Only he's got kids, so if we fired him—" Toshi said, but my foot crunched on the ground, and, all at once, they turned to me. She leaned forward and frowned. "I keep hoping he'll change."

"Where did Tan go?" I said.

"He left."

Someone started yelling. Kazuo, who was the boss of the group, was coming out of the hatchery with Nori and Mr. Tanizaki. Mr. Tanizaki was still carrying on about a car. "If I want to talk about a car, I'll talk about a car, and that's all there is to it."

Kazuo said something quietly to him.

Mr. Tanizaki answered loudly. "I can talk and work at the same time. I'm no moron."

Kazuo raised his voice for the first time. "You straighten out now or go home."

Nori just stood. He hadn't said a word. He faced the highway as if he saw something interesting there. I turned to the highway, and when I turned back, a half second later, Nori was facing Mr. Tanizaki with his arms crossed over his chest and his feet planted wide. Mr. Tanizaki had his hands at his sides, and he was opening and closing his fists. Tension spread out like a wave, until it touched me.

"It's amazing the way the clouds have cleared up," I said. I felt as if I half shouted, yet my voice came out flimsy, brittle. But the three men heard and looked my way. Kazuo put his hand on Mr. Tanizaki's shoulder, and everyone returned to work.

Later that night, the other inoculators finished and went home, and I went to bed in my sleeping bag. I was too tired to think or worry. All I could think about was what I was doing at each moment: I'm arranging a pillow; I'm turning off the light; I'm closing my eyes. The sexers woke me up in a few hours, when they came into the room to sleep. Nori set the radio on a counter. There was a commercial on: "Lars soap is best; it'll pass the test." Mr. Tanizaki made a pun to Toshi, who'd just dropped cigarette ash on her pants. "Don't burn your britches," he said. "Bridges? Britches?" He nodded seriously. Sometimes, when he and my father were telling jokes, my father would get hysterical with laughter, while

Mr. Tanizaki would smile, without laughing, and nod his head more and more furiously. So now, after he made his pun, he nodded his head sharply a few times and Toshi looked worried.

A couple of people took Valiums. Eight clocks ticked in the room. Once before when we'd stayed overnight, there'd been only one clock, and it failed to go off. Now each person wanted to be responsible for the time, just in case. The clocks glowed different colors, pale greens, pale oranges, and whites, and when I woke up I opened my eyes to see a green clock face vibrating in the dark as it rang. Seven other clocks went off in succession.

Tan was already there, helping pull newborn chicks from the incubators. The day went without incident, and after work I headed directly to the car. I never liked to wait around. I didn't mind being inside, where I was sure I heard chirping, and I didn't mind being near the car, where I was too far away to hear. But near the door, I couldn't be sure whether I barely heard chirping or whether there was residual sound echoing in my ears, like an afterimage when you close your eyes.

Tan and I got into the car with his father. When Mr. Tanizaki hit the highway, he pressed hard on the accelerator. Fence posts whizzed by. We were heading toward the Tanizakis' town—I think he'd forgotten about driving me home.

I felt I was in the way. "Discard me anywhere," I said.

We drove quietly for a few more minutes. *"Dad,"* said Tan.

Mr. Tanizaki lifted his foot somewhat from the accelerator, and we got pulled forward as the car slowed down.

"We have to take her home," said Tan. The way he said "her" instead of my name made me aware of what I was just then, a minor player. Mr. Tanizaki eyed me with dull curiosity.

Tan leaned across me and touched his father's arm. *"Dad.* Why don't I drive?"

Mr. Tanizaki pulled over, and the two of them got out and changed places.

We drove into my town a new way, past a rusted pink-and-gray trailer with an American flag flying in front; past a wooden church with a YES, WE'RE OPEN sign on the front door; past fields and fences, just a few miles from my home, that I had never seen. A number of old houses had been torn down in the last couple of years, and we passed several lots where all that remained were splintered planks shooting up from the grass. The sights weren't really much different from the sights the way we usually went, but Gibson seemed very mysterious to me at that moment.

Mr. Tanizaki studied his hands sadly. Tan was paler than I'd ever seen him. I had a weird feeling. I thought, I love being here. I think it was sort of like when someone you love has been hurt, and despite how awful it is, there's still that part inside you that feels incredibly lucky to love the person, even as you feel hurt yourself.

When we got to my house, Mr. Tanizaki went inside to talk to my father. I heard one of my brothers yelling, "No, it's *your* turn to set the table and *my* turn to make the salad." Tan and I meandered along the highway, stopping at a large house. Outside hung a sign, ROCKS, MINERALS & SOUVENIRS, and there was a table covered with colored stones and hardened wood. We threw a few of the rocks at some trees, then put money on the table under some wood. After we returned to my place, we hung around out back, standing against the wall of my house and kissing very hard, our bodies pressed into each other, until it almost hurt.

"Let's go," Mr. Tanizaki called, and Tan went around front. I tasted a little bit of blood, where my teeth had just now cut into the inside of my mouth.

I went to bed right after supper. It was not yet dark, and distorted gray sky shone through some jars sitting on the windowsill. Walker had put them there. They were filled with chrysalises and caterpillars he'd collected. At first he would collect his insects and put them on his own windowsill, but when he ran out of room, he placed the jars all over the house, as if they were flower vases. He was always searching for jars in those days, and my parents even bought him some for his eleventh birthday. To make jars empty more quickly, he consumed astonishing amounts of mayonnaise. He put it on his pancakes, on his scrambled eggs, and in his vegetable soup. He claimed the caterpillars would never leave an uncovered jar if they had enough food, though one morning I stepped out of bed and just missed squashing a large green caterpillar. Now I listened as a caterpillar occasionally lost its footing, as it were, and a twig snapped. I was used to the sound but tonight found it unsettling—odd and dreamlike.

Tan and Mr. Tanizaki picked me up for work at four the next morning. I watched their headlights slant across the living room draperies and ran to the door.

My father called out, "Can't sleep. I'll walk you outside." I knew he must have been waiting for Mr. Tanizaki, too.

Outside, the air was crisp, and the houses were devoid of life. My father opened the car door and leaned in.

"Can't sleep," he said.

"You look good for a man who can't sleep," said Mr. Tanizaki.

Charlie-O guffawed. "Even when I'm looking good I don't look so good." Mr. Tanizaki rubbed his chin and appeared to be considering my father's words. He revved up the motor, and my father hesitated before stepping aside and letting me in. "You drive carefully," he yelled out as we drove off. He was still watching, barefoot and in pajamas, when we turned the corner. As we moved out of sight, I think I heard him another time: "You drive that car carefully!"

At the hatchery, the sexers worked through the day, slept, and worked again, and it was dark once more when they finished. Then they held a meeting that Tan was allowed to attend but I wasn't.

I waited outside. The woman who acted as my boss was leaving, but she didn't acknowledge me as she passed. She tripped on the dirt drive, and as she regained her balance she instinctively started to turn her head, to see whether I'd noticed her trip, but she caught herself before turning all the way. As she continued to walk, I could tell by a rigidity in one of her legs that she'd hurt herself but didn't want me to know and hoped I wasn't watching. I turned away.

The sexers began coming out of the hatchery. "A good day," Nori said. "The chicks weren't too wet to handle and they weren't too dry."

Nori, Kazuo, and the others stood outside, loitering, which they never did, and I knew Mr. Tanizaki had been fired. When he came out with Tan, the talking ceased. Tan stood very straight, very proud, by the door. His father wore a strange expression, as if he'd just gone deaf, as if all the noise in the world had stopped, all those small noises in the trees, and voices, and cars.

Toshi was the first to go over to speak to Mr. Tanizaki. I heard her say "Good luck." She spoke kindly, but she'd probably worn her impassive face inside, when she was voting to fire Mr. Tanizaki. He looked at her and blinked. Still deaf. Nori and Kazuo shook his hand and mumbled things I couldn't hear. Then Nori came by and tweaked my nose. Kazuo and Nori walked over to a car and just stood around. It occurred to me that their coolness and toughness hid an awkwardness they all felt with each other, and I really was one of them: being one of them was being an outsider. To be part of their group, you couldn't get close to them.

The street inclined, and every so often an automobile came up the incline, but the drivers paid no attention to the hatchery as they drove by. With the approach of each vehicle, the car light dispersed slowly throughout the air. The breeze was strong and then soft, rhythmic, and I thought how if Mr. Tanizaki were really deaf he might be extra aware of the wind, playing like music against his skin. He and Tan walked out under some trees. Tan lit a cigarette, which he shared with his father. Tall maples around them bloomed toward the black sky. The only color was the orange ash when someone inhaled from the cigarette.

My family had lived many places, and traveled many places. I thought then that Arkansas was the most beautiful place I had ever been in, yet I wanted badly to leave, and I knew that, unlike Toshi and Nori and Kazuo—and even my father, committed now to his garage—someday I would have that freedom.

13

☙☙ I helped Tan and his family pack when Mr. Tanizaki found a new job in Indiana. It was a temporary move for Tan. The rest of his family was going to settle down, but he was going to leave for college a year later; he got good grades and wanted to go to a school in the Northeast. I expected to go in California; I didn't get good enough grades to attend a great school, but I planned to attend a state school after living with an aunt in Los Angeles for a year.

The night we packed, Tan came by after I'd gone to sleep. He called at my window, and we took a blanket into the trees. It would have been romantic, but a tick jumped into his ear and later we got rained out. Then, as I was climbing back through the window after saying good-bye for the last time, I slipped on the wet sill and fell into the mud with a wonderful suctiony sound. It was okay with me. The thing about our sex life was it made us feel close, not because it was romantic or beautiful or sweet or anything like that (although at times it was all of those), but mainly because it was a prodigious adventure we were going through together.

Without Tan, the school year was just all right—not great, not awful. I worked part time at the hatchery but then got another job, keeping an elderly man company three times a week. I read to him, listened to the radio with him, cleaned for him. We used to spend hours together raking leaves quietly, even going beyond his property, just for the pleasure of raking. His property was full of trees, and leaves would be spread all over, varying in color from the reds and golds of autumn to pastel greens, the leaves seemingly encompassing all seasons at once. For a while he was feuding with all his relatives, and I was his best friend. I worked for him only a few months; he's an elusive memory now, yet I was really fond of him. Sometimes, on hard days, I think about what a happy but small part of my life that was, and I start to feel waves of sadness arising from the loss of something so sweet and transient.

The only other things that stand out about my last year in Arkansas are my good-bye party and the time my father's name appeared in the newspaper. He and some of his friends had been part of what my mother called a gambling ring, though my father said the so-called gambling ring was really "just a few guys with a bookie." One day the police arrested the bookie and some of his clients, and the newspaper named my father as among those arrested. The police also arrested four of my father's closest friends: Teddy Kitano, Satoru Morita, Izzy Watanabe, and Ruby Tanaka. I thought the arrests were a big deal at the time, but a couple of years ago when I looked at the newspaper clipping, I saw it was only three paragraphs long. According to the story, the bookie was arrested every year. "It's become sort of a tradition," said the chief of police. "One year we arrested the mayor, this year we decided to arrest a bunch of Japs." The whole affair caused quite a stir among my father and his friends. They thought they would be run out of town. When I was older and listened to them discuss the arrests, I could still hear in their voices something of the distress they'd felt, and once in a while I felt it, too. I doubt, though, that anyone besides us really cared or remembered.

In any case, when I left for Los Angeles, it was my parents' friends—Teddy, Satoru, Izzy, Ruby, and others—whom we invited to the going-away party. We held the party in August, the night before I left to stay with my Aunt Lily and her family.

Walker helped me decorate the house with colored paper,

and I helped him hang a ten-foot-long good-bye sign he'd made for me. It's not that I loved Walker the most—I loved all my brothers the same—but I thought the most about Walker, if only because he was thin and sad and sensitive, and he worried me.

At seven o'clock my parents and I waited outside for their friends. Though it was still light, the hills already looked black. To the side, the sign from Monty's Bar and Grill rose off the highway. I could view the sign from my bedroom; sometimes it was the last thing I saw before I fell asleep. There were three other houses on our stretch of road. Next door was the Nolans'. They had a lot of kids, but we never got to know them. One of the boys always used to be pulling his pants down in front of strangers, and my father wouldn't allow us to talk to any of the Nolans, though you couldn't help peeking out the window sometimes. Down the street lived the Stemmlers. They had no children, and I didn't know much about them. On holidays they exchanged pastries with my family, which was kind of silly since none of us from either family could cook well; but my father thought it was a nice gesture. The house across the street was empty now. A series of migrant families had lived there over the years. Walker used to think it was the same family living there all that time. He had suspected it was sort of a ghost family; he'd somehow extrapolated hauntings from poverty, maybe because he was scared of both. Anyway, that was the neighborhood I was leaving.

I always think of my going-away party not just as the night before I left Arkansas but also as the night Walker disappeared. Of course, he had disappeared before, but for some reason that night it was different.

As my parents and I waited for guests, Ben and Walker ran through the front yard.

"No one's coming to your party," Ben yelled, to tease me.

"No one's coming to your party," Walker said. He was a master at mimicking all of us, but he excelled at doing Ben.

"Anyhow," said my father, "read some good books for

me. I never have time.'' He paused, and I could tell he was searching his mind. My parents were full of advice for me lately. "Read Charles Dickens," he finally added, triumphantly.

"Do you think?" said my mother. "If she reads too much she'll hurt her eyes and get headaches and ruin her good nature." I saw my father look sideways at her, like: What good nature? My mother turned to me. "You can read a lot the second year if you like. Read the Existentialists. The first year, just read what you have to. Have a good time."

"Stop copying me," said Ben.

"Stop copying me," said Walker.

"Ahhh, I can't stand this."

Ben tore off down the road. Walker chased him, shouting, "Ahhh, I can't stand this."

My dress rustled every time the wind blew. It was a blue cotton dress with an ivory lace collar. It wasn't formal, but it was too nice for school or even for the sort of parties I'd been invited to the past year, and this was the first time I'd worn it, except in my room. It was the first dress I'd ever bought with my own money.

We'd lined our windowsills with tangerines and pounded rice cakes, the way my mother said her mother always had on New Year's Eve when she was little. Everyone kept eating the fruit, so all night the house smelled of tangerines.

My brothers were going to be allowed to stay up as late as they wanted, but they mostly hid in the hall and peeked in, just as if they were sneaking. I got sort of drunk and walked around laughing at anything anyone said, even serious things. I was full of opinions for a while, about books and movies and whatever anyone was talking about. It was getting late when Ben came into the room and said Walker had gone down to the vending machine at the gas station a mile away to get candy but he'd never returned. That, Ben said, had been more than an hour ago. Everybody searched all over and couldn't find Walker, and when my mother called the gas station, the attendant said he was getting ready to close up and hadn't seen anyone.

Ruby Tanaka raised his beer bottle, stood up, and said, "Charge! Let's go find him!"

I turned to my father. He had a cool, almost calculating look in his eyes.

"I hope nobody did anything to him!" said Ruby.

I figured Walker had just wandered off the way he always did, but we decided to go searching for him. I accompanied my father, Izzy, and Vince—the blackjack dealer—in one direction; Ruby and a few people searched in the opposite direction. When I looked back, I saw some of them picking up rocks and pieces of wood. The Stemmlers' curtain moved. They must have been watching from inside their dark house. I stood still a moment to try to see them. Perhaps they were scared of us. I felt suddenly scared myself: what if they called the police and my father got arrested again? I reached out for him, but he was already way ahead; I hurried to catch up.

We walked through a field. You could see the hills from where we walked—two flashlights made splinters of light in their blackness. Far off, it was thundering, but it hadn't started to rain. The night seemed unusually quiet, as if all the crickets who made a racket most evenings had deserted Gibson. I felt scared again, but this time it was a fear that seemed to rise from the past, as if we were not now walking through the outskirts of Gibson in the twentieth century but instead were searching for someone hundreds of years earlier, and we were full of the inevitable fears and necessary courage I imagined people possessed back then. I started thinking how Walker never wandered off this late. All my brothers could be reckless, but mainly during the day. I picked up a rock. My father found a thick piece of wood somewhere. He looked tiny against the fields stretched out around us. He and Izzy walked ahead, with Vince and me following. It had started to rain, the drops like static over the fields. There was something strangely erotic in the fear in the air; it drew me to Vince. For a moment I rested my hand on his back, ostensibly to keep my balance. It was like when you put your hand to a window, and your hand can feel how it is on the other side, whether it's windy or still. I could feel inside him: he felt something in the air, too. My father turned suddenly to wait. He hesitated, then said brusquely that we ought to hurry.

"This field goes on until the highway curves through it," I said.

"Do the boys ever come out this far?"

"I doubt Walker would come out here tonight. But if someone did something to him . . ." I started to cry. I hadn't even known I wanted to cry.

We continued to the highway, stopping sometimes to look through bushes, and then headed back to the house. Several women were huddled in the front yard under umbrellas like huge colored mushrooms. My father, Izzy, and Vince left again immediately, and my mother and I went in.

Peter had fallen asleep in the living room. A baseball bat leaned against him as he slept—he'd been scared, too. I sat on the floor and laid my head on the couch. The rain fell in a sudden spurt on the front porch. I noticed I was still carrying a rock. I felt sleepy and alert at the same time.

The couch shook, so I looked up. Ben was smirking.

"What's with you?" I said.

He suppressed a giggle. When the phone rang, he jumped up and laughed. I knew the call would be about Walker. In a moment my mother was crying out, "He's with Bill and Susan. He's with Bill and Susan." Bill and Susan Yokoyama. I went into the kitchen. My mother said Walker had hidden in their car when they'd left, then stayed awhile, for the comic effect.

Back in the living room, Peter was still sleeping. Ben turned on the television. I turned it off. "Get to bed before I flatten you," I said. "And take Peter."

The Yokoyamas didn't live far. When they brought Walker back he looked proud of himself and didn't understand why everyone was so mad at him. My mother's sister, who was visiting, said she had half a mind to box his ears, but then she hugged him so hard he cried out.

"You get to go away," he said to me. "So I thought, Why couldn't I, just for a while?"

"You know, I can't wait to get away from all of you," I said. His face fell, and I felt instantly sorry, but I didn't show it. I waited at the front window, mostly for my father and Vince to get back. The hills were black again; everyone must have been searching the other side. My mother came up and put her arm around me. "Walker's too old for nonsense like this, but in a way I'm glad at least he wasn't around tonight." Later I decided she'd meant she was glad that at least Walker hadn't needed to be scared like the rest of us.

When my father returned and saw Walker, his face took on a singular expression, confused and overwhelmingly relieved. It was as if at that moment the expression became etched permanently on his face, because even today when he hasn't seen one of us for a long time, I see remnants of the same confusion and relief.

Some of the men went to work getting drunk for real now. Izzy passed out, lying half on my father's favorite chair and half on the floor. Now and then he came to life and took a swig from his bottle. He also roused himself every so often to say, "Long live college." His wife looked alternately embarrassed and proud of his brio. Izzy was my father's great friend, the one he owned the garage with. They'd worked the fields together in California as children, and they'd lived next door to each other in Little Tokyo in Los Angeles way before the area became a ghost town during the war.

The party ended a couple of hours later, when everyone was thoroughly drunk and my mother decided she'd had enough. Everyone shook my hand, kissed my cheek, and left. Vince did just like everyone else. But then he leaned in again and whispered, "You'll do great." That made me feel good. I had talked to him a couple of times at parties. He would tell me who in his life he had cared about and why, and who he had not cared about and why not. I thought—at the time—that he had known many people, and many different kinds of people. At the time, everything he said was interesting to me. I figured everyone in the world came through the casino where he worked.

"A lot of excitement, but I guess that doesn't change anything for you," my father was saying. "I guess you're still leaving later."

My father and I couldn't sleep, so we cleaned up and decided to go down to Monty's. The sky was getting light. There was something almost violet, something lovely and soft, in the sky and the street. It seemed ridiculous to me that a few hours earlier we'd been not only worried but very scared. And of what? It had actually crossed my mind that one of my neighbors had done something to Walker. Now even the fluorescent lights of the restaurant seemed warmer than usual. The few other customers watched us with blank faces, but feeling suddenly lighthearted, I smiled at them. I *was* leaving later.

My father and I took a booth. He picked up a packet of sugar and turned it over in his hands. His hands were deceptively thick and dark; I knew they were agile. The blue veins stood out like welts.

The waitress, Sandra, came over. She had a blond beehive set on her red hair. On top of the beehive was her yellow waitress cap. "Long time no see," she said.

"She's going away to college today," said my father. Actually, that wasn't strictly true. I wasn't planning to start school for another year. He was not lying, just proud.

Sandra nodded seriously. "So you have a brain after all. I always thought you might. Sue and Lenora from the lunch shift said no way does that Livvie have a brain, but I said, You never know. Anything's possible."

"Thank you," I said, feeling pleased with myself.

I rarely ordered coffee in restaurants, so that's what I asked for, part of the new, sophisticated me. She scribbled that down. "No, maybe orange juice instead." I didn't really like coffee very much. She erased. "Oh, no, I want to stay awake. I have lots to do. Coffee, please."

Sandra sighed as she scribbled, erased, scribbled. She had a thick Southern drawl. "Like I always tell my husband," she said, "you're cute, but you put me through too many changes." She went to get our order.

My father knocked his thick knuckles against his lips. The

restaurant shook as a truck drove by. "I made a mistake," he said. "We should have called Susan and Bill as soon as we couldn't find Walker."

"We had no reason to think he would be with them."

"See, I try to get through every day without making any mistakes."

"What?"

"You probably wouldn't understand." Another singular expression passed over his face, not of hate, really—at least, not of hate toward me. But, maybe, of resentment. I had never noticed him looking that way before, and it made me feel defensive, and then sad for just a few of the things that bound my family together: fears, resentments, necessities.

He leaned forward. "Take the garage for an example. I try to be exact. I don't want to use any more movement than I have to when I'm fixing a car. I look at it and make my decisions as quickly as possible, then do everything I have to do—get my tools and so forth—with the least possible movement. I want to be perfect. Don't you ever want to be perfect?" His voice sounded monotonous, automatic. I realized how hard this night had been on him. "When we were searching for Walker, I didn't feel anything. In the same way, all day my whole mind is focused just on what I'm doing. When I'm fixing a car, or, say, working in the garden for hours, my hands become what most people's hearts are. They feel for me. That's a trick I learned in the army, how to let my hands feel for me. So *I* don't have to feel anything."

Sandra, sensing a change at our table, brought our coffee quietly and left. I tried to understand what my father was saying, but I felt so sleepy. Instead I stared at his ugly hands and had a feeling almost of awe at the weight they had carried.

"In case you ever wondered what I do all day," said my father.

My family had taken good care of our home. Today it had a neatly trimmed lawn in front and a swing set in the large backyard. During the first summer, I used to pull the centers out of honeysuckle flowers and suck the sweetness, or else chew lamb's-leaves, those tangy sour plants that grew wild and looked like clover. The first summer we'd moved to Gibson, I'd played alone a lot. I caught bumblebees in my mother's gold-plated change case or collected stones in coffee cans. Evenings, we might take quilts into our backyard. Sitting beneath the Milky Way, we talked of everyday things—friends and meals and work. Other nights we sat silently. On those quiet nights, we would sit within a few feet of each other, but we each felt free to dream as we pleased.

That's what I thought about later as we drove to the next town so I could catch the bus. Waiting at the station was a young couple with a baby, and two men who looked in their twenties. One had a crew cut, the other wore his hair slicked back.

My father eyed both of them suspiciously. I knew what he was thinking: I hope she has the good sense to sit near the front of the bus.

Ben was swinging a neck chain in his hand. At the end of the chain hung what looked like a clear white shell.

"Where did you get that shell?" said my father absently.

"Don't you remember? That's from last year when I tripped on a hoe and ripped off the nail from my big toe."

My father started, as if someone had just splashed water on him.

My mother began to sob. "Don't get fat," she said. "Men don't like that."

I got on the bus and smelled exhaust, air-conditioning, cigarette smoke, and the provocative unfamiliar scents of people I'd never met. I was glad to leave my parents. That was one of the things they didn't know about me. I was already full of beliefs, assumptions, and feelings that many years later I would want badly to unlearn. My parents had taught me many things they hadn't meant to teach me and I hadn't meant to learn. One of those things was fear; their first big fear, during the war; and when my father was arrested; their fear when Walker was missing; concern that I would be all right in the future; and a hundred other inter-woven fears. That was what I wanted to leave.

I always thought I'd tell my mother how I'd seen Obāsan die. But now as I was leaving, I saw such a confession as more a burden to my mother than my own absolution. The bus drove through the hills. I had forty hours to daydream before I reached my new home.

※ *14*

※※ In Oklahoma, a boy boarded who said he raised boa constrictors for a living. He had a loud, happy voice and a huge cowboy hat. No one believed him at first, so he took a bag down from the luggage rack and showed the other passengers two snakes; he said he had more snakes below, as well as some rats. He was going to Hollywood because a famous singer-actor wanted to buy a boa from him. He looked about my age and said he lived alone in Oklahoma. He kept trying to make friends with the other passengers by offering them Kool-Aid from a big jug. "I don't like the stuff myself, but I thought I'd bring some in case anyone else got thirsty." He kept trying to talk to a pretty girl in front. He asked her repeatedly what kind of boys she liked, and finally she said, "I like boys who aren't phony and don't brag a lot. I like natural boys." Then she looked out the window.

A couple from Sweden gave me a book to read before they got off.

An ex-coastguardsman gave me a green glass fishing weight he'd found on a beach in Alaska, where he'd once been stationed. It was quiet and empty there, he said, and sometimes he saw polar bears when he walked in the morning.

During a rest stop, I sat and talked with a prostitute, who was really sweet and reminded me of the nurse I had when they took out my tonsils. When a friend came to pick her up, the friend asked me whether I worked at the same place. I said, No, I worked somewhere else. They smiled and left.

I took my bags outside and sat on the raised area beneath a lamppost and a tree. Every time the wind blew hard, leaves fell on me. The sky was cloudless. I closed my eyes but opened them with a start and checked my purse: I kept feeling nervous about losing my money. But the money—about twenty dollars, plus a check for my savings—was still there, along with some coupons my mother had slipped in my wallet. She had put gold stars on the coupons she thought I might need most, tampons and cereal.

When we got on the bus again, the air conditioner broke down. A baby didn't stop crying until the final overhead light was turned out. From the back came the rustling and groans of two people making love. In front, the pretty girl and a boy giggled. The sound of lovemaking made me feel lonely and also amorous. I scrunched my thighs closer together.

Outside, clouds like spots made the sky look like the hide of an animal. The moon was a thin crescent between two spots. Rising from the blackness beneath them was a mass of thin lighted pipes pointing out in all directions from a large white metal center. It was a factory, lit by greenish fluorescence. There was nothing out there but the black flatness and the explosion of greenish lights. "My husband works there," said the woman next to me. She got off at the next stop.

Blackness again. I thought I saw a hitchhiker materialize beside the road, but he vanished just as quickly.

There was so much that I wanted. That's what kept welling up in me, disturbing my sleeping and waking dreams.

The woman with the baby and the man who'd been making love in back got off in Flagstaff, Arizona, and so did an ex-marine I'd talked to earlier. The woman who'd been making love and the pretty girl got off in Barstow, California, with three other people. In Los Angeles, I got off with the boa constrictor boy and several others. The boy walked off alone. He still had his jug of red Kool-Aid, and it was still full.

.

✵✵ 15

✵✵ After I left Gibson, I lived a disorderly life, not from any spirit of rebellion, nor from any coherent philosophy, but simply because I didn't yet realize there were other ways of living. The plan was for me to stay with my Aunt Lily for a year so I could gain residency in California and pay lower tuition. But I ended up staying only a couple of months before I got my own apartment. I was scared to tell my parents when I decided to move out, but they weren't surprised. My mother said the older she got, the harder it was to surprise her, and my father said not to tell my mother, but he'd never liked Aunt Lily much, anyhow.

Money wasn't really a problem. As soon as I arrived in Los Angeles I found a salesgirl job at a lamp shop in Beverly Hills, and I'd spent hardly any of my savings from the hatchery.

My apartment sat near a freeway; from the kitchen window you could see cars flickering between the hedges. The apartment was two small rooms with old brown carpeting, and a brown-carpeted staircase heading toward the ceiling from the middle of the living room floor. My landlady didn't know why the stairs were there—she'd bought the building the way it was. I used the staircase for plants, books, and baskets, and I drew pictures of it to send my parents. Actually, my only books were my grandmother's diaries, which I was still reading, and my only plants were two pots of fake gardenias my aunt had lent me.

My apartment complex, seven buildings of eight studios each, was white stucco, like most other apartments on the block. The trees lining the street always seemed to have yellowing leaves, giving an impression not just of dryness but of age. But I didn't notice how old they looked until later, when I moved out.

Every evening when I got home from work, the sound of electric guitars cut through the dry air, Chuck Berry riffs over and over from an apartment in back, until you figured it was all the player knew, which I learned later it wasn't. He could play classical very well but hardly ever did. There were a number of down-and-out musicians around, and someone was always playing. The landlady didn't allow anyone to play after ten, so when the music stopped, I always knew the time.

The apartment complex was part of what one of my neighbors called the entertainment-industry culture of failure that existed in Los Angeles. Most of the complex's occupants fell into two categories: young and old. The old were people who'd lived there for years and couldn't afford to move. Some of them had me over for dinner sometimes and told stories about how they used to be songwriters or screenwriters or nightclub owners. Very few women lived alone in the area, and once in a while if some of the guys got drunk they'd come pounding on my door or the door of another girl, until an old couple who lived downstairs chased them away with a BB gun.

Aunt Lily called me every day for a month, saying I ought to move back in with her family. But I liked where I lived. It gave me that old feeling of being displaced and safe at the same time, like when I used to play in the small woods back of my house at night. I could close my eyes and from any point at the edge find my way to a certain tree in the center.

My first boyfriend in Los Angeles lived a few buildings down. His name was Andy Chin, and he wrecked cars for a living. Now and then, he worked in the Hollywood Hills. I don't mean he worked a crane in a junkyard or anything. I mean people paid him to wreck cars, for insurance reasons, or because they were mad at their ex-spouses; things like that. If they told him what the reason was, fine; if not, that was fine, too. I've never really known any other professional criminals. I was surprised when I found out what he did, because he seemed earnest, not a hustler at all. Really, I thought wrecking cars was simply what he did for now, just as I worked at a lamp shop.

Andy was medium height, and thin, with horn-rimmed glasses. Though he was Chinese, he looked sort of like Buddy Holly. The first time I talked to him was one morning when I went downstairs and found him examining a dent in my car. It was an old, cheap car and didn't seem to me worth fixing. The morning haze had barely burned off, and the sky was a sweet almost-blue. Andy was bending over, his back to me. "It's not for sale," I said.

He turned and scrutinized me critically as if I, too, were a dent in a car—a bad dent. "I sure wouldn't want it if it was."

"I'm not looking for anyone to fix it, either. I can't afford it."

"*I* don't repair cars." He sounded affronted.

"What's wrong with repairing cars?" I said, myself affronted.

He ignored the question. He looked two or three years older than I was, but he already had a streak of gray in his black hair. "You weren't moving, were you?"

"Huh?"

"At the time of the accident?"

"No, I was waiting at the intersection to make a left, and someone going straight hit me."

He spaced out, and seemed to be envisioning the accident. "And the car that hit you was powder blue, going maybe thirty miles an hour?"

I perked up. "Are you a private detective?"

I waited. "I work with cars," he said. I liked him. He had a funny way of moving, as if he were lighter than everyone else, his whole body but especially his hands and arms existing in their own private gravity.

I drove off to work and didn't see Andy again until one morning several days later. He was leaning against my car and seemed to be waiting for me. I looked at him suspiciously. "Are you sure you're not looking for a repair job?"

"I just felt like talking. Where do you go, all dressed up?"

"I work at this fancy-shmancy lamp shop."

"How much does a fancy-schmancy lamp cost?"

"Some of them are cheap when they're on sale, sixty dollars or so, and some are as much as several thousand dollars. There's this great one, green glass, that was designed by a famous lamp guy from the forties. It costs four hundred. I'm saving for it." Later Andy told me that was the dumbest thing he'd ever heard, but he didn't say so at the time, to spare my feelings. He said my wanting the lamp reminded him of those women who work for minimum wage in boutiques and spend all their money on their hair, makeup, and clothes.

He looked admiringly toward the freeway for a moment, then laughed. "Cars are something else."

It took him a while, but after we'd been seeing each other a few months, he told me what he really did. I think I asked so many questions he suspected me of wanting to report him. I was just curious; he was mysterious to me. I thought he was sweet and funny, which seemed strange for a guy who wrecked cars.

Andy's only repeat employer was a rich man from Encino. His name was Roger, and three or four times he asked Andy to stage a fake accident: hitting an expensive car—a Rolls-Royce or Mercedes registered in Roger's name—with a junker. The repair bill might be anywhere between five and twenty-five thousand dollars. I never really understood how it worked—wouldn't the authorities get suspicious about his repeated insurance claims?—but I think Roger would have his attorney instruct the insurance agent to send the check to him rather than the repair man, and later Roger would deny he received the check or ever asked anyone to fix the car in the first place. Roger was probably involved in other insurance frauds, as well, because Andy once said he kept a whole filing cabinet filled with information about insurance companies and their agents. The money from the wrecked cars would have been a very small part of his business. I knew Roger had been in jail and felt confident he wouldn't ever have to go back, but that's all I knew.

I saw Roger once. Andy pointed him out to me inside a tailor's. The tailor was trying to measure him, but he kept interrupting to show the tailor handkerchief tricks. Andy said he loved to perform tricks, sometimes the same one over and over.

All this was very amazing, even funny, to me. It's like when you go to an aquarium and marvel at the strangest fish. I liked knowing about this secret world. It was sort of like knowing about the hatchery. Hanging around with Andy was probably a bad choice, but I really liked him.

Besides Roger, Andy's customers were people who found him by referral. A surprising number of his customers were women. "I guess if the guys want to wreck a car, they mostly do it themselves." Men or women, some of his customers liked to tell him their secrets and problems. They would try to justify their wanting a car wrecked, as if they needed his approval. Other customers insisted on elaborate plans to avoid identifying themselves. Sometimes they even used disguises. Once, a man's fake mustache fell off during a transaction.

Now and then, people would want him to wreck a car out of their neighborhoods; that is, he would have to steal the car, take it into the hills, wreck it, and bring it back. The only time he took me with him was a year after we'd met. When I'd first moved to L.A., I'd planned to start school by then, but I put it off.

We drove deep into the hills in a green Pontiac, and a friend of his drove a Ford. They were going to take care of two customers at once. We went to an isolated point high up. You could see a section of the flat city, a sheet of lights fading into the darkness of the ocean.

Another girl had come. She had a fresh, cool face and a

big cheerleader's smile. She said she always came on these expeditions in case her boyfriend got hurt. We watched Andy and his friend discussing tactics.

"He's cute," she said, referring to Andy.

"Uh-huh."

"How long have you known him?" It was as if we were on a double date at the soda fountain.

"A year."

"He must really trust you. I don't think he ever brought a girl here before."

"They're okay for cheap cars," Andy was saying. He patted the Ford affectionately.

This was going to be a complicated procedure, because they wanted to damage one of the cars more badly than the other. They were discussing whether to collide the cars, scrape one against a tree before colliding them, or just ram them both into a tree. Andy's friend was sitting on the driver's side of the Ford, while Andy leaned against the car, talking to him. The inside car light was on, and the headlights from the Pontiac were shining on them. The Ford seemed to be glowing organically. It was like that Magritte painting where it's day and night at the same time. The cars seemed to be in day, surrounded by night. They decided to sideswipe the cars and if necessary scrape one on a tree. Once they'd made their decision, their faces changed, as if they were boxers after the bell.

The girl stood beside me, her arms hugging her abdomen. Andy backed up, the cars scraped, and in the abrupt silence afterward a piece of chrome plunked to the ground. I didn't move for a second but then ran forward. Andy and his friend were fine, though. Andy got out, and we sat near the edge of the hill. His friend took a piece of fender and heaved it over; it glimmered once and merged with the city lights. "Crash!" he yelled. "Kaboom!"

"He's enthusiastic," I said to Andy.

"He's nuts. Like he's seen *King Kong* seventeen times."

I thought about their faces when they were working, about the awful scrape of the cars, and about the abrupt silence.

"That was really weird." Andy looked unhappy now, very tense. A broken-off branch touched his arm, and he jumped. I wanted to draw him out of this mood.

"I got a letter from one of my uncles today," I said chirpily. "We write about once a year."

Andy nodded. I got the feeling he was in pain. "Did you hurt yourself?"

"No," he said. He didn't feel like talking, but I could tell he was going to indulge me. "So . . . So what's your uncle like?"

"He's okay. You get used to him, even though he's kind of bossy. When I was in a quiet mood, he used to tell me he could see the wheels turning inside. 'Speak up! Speak up! Don't be afraid of my station!' Really I'd just be daydreaming or thinking about TV or something."

He ran his hand through his hair. He looked very drained and spoke to me now while staring out toward the ocean. "So what did your uncle say in the letter?"

"He just talked about his former wife. They'd opened this fat farm in Kentucky—*Vogue* has called it the most economical spa in America—and they argued so much about it, they ended up divorcing. They had a big fight about whether they should put in a soft-drink machine or stick to juices. Uncle Roy said soft drinks, his wife said juices. She got the farm after they divorced, and now she's ended up getting a Coke machine. He just wrote me that." Andy didn't say anything. I wondered sometimes about his own past, and about his relatives. He said he hardly ever talked to his parents. He was examining a twig, but his face still held some of the harshness from earlier. A sudden feeling overwhelmed me. "I hated you while you were doing that," I said, but he didn't answer.

His friend was beating his chest and howling at the half-moon, which was huge, and yellow the way very old paper is. Andy put his arm around me, sort of protecting me from something, but also as if I were protecting him. After a while we got in one of the cars and went home, leaving his friend still howling at the moon.

* * *

Andy's apartment had a stained olive-green carpet, a bed that pulled out of the wall, a coffee table and a plaid sofa that came with the place, and windows through whose cracks the air whistled or hooted or sang, depending on the strength of the breeze. If you strained out the bathroom window and it wasn't too smoggy, you could see the serene, light-sprinkled Hollywood Hills. The only items in the apartment belonging to Andy were three fish tanks sitting across from the bed.

We made love twice that night. The first time was sort of rough, the second time was different, sort of quietly intense. Before we made love the second time, his hand lay for a long while against my throat before moving over my breasts. His mouth rested, momentarily, on my breasts, on my shoulders, against my face.

Later I found myself hypnotized by his fish tanks: the blue trees, the green pebbles, the red-orange fish. He kept his fish in the house because he believed they sopped up evil spirits. When a fish died, it was because it had soaked up too much evil. Next to me, Andy's face was in the pillow. There were two rotating fans, and every few seconds they crossed over us. Sometimes, when we'd just had a fight, we kept the fans on even when it got cool, to fill the silence.

Lately, I'd had an awareness of myself, of the texture and smell of my hair and skin, the length and strength of my muscles; and now, superimposed on my own body, I felt the outlines of Andy, an invisible presence resting inside me. It was almost like being pregnant, as if he were growing inside. I even dreamed something Andy sometimes did, that several fish died. I woke up to what I thought was a noise downstairs and stuck my head out the door. The door across the hall opened and I and the old man who lived across the way stood face to face, everything but the man's head hidden behind his door. I saw that behind his placid facade he was scared. We looked at each other for a moment, then downstairs, before the man closed the door. But I knew he was listening, scared, behind his door.

Someone *was* making noise from below. Sometimes people sat outside this late, but I saw only one person downstairs now—Henry, who lived in the building in back, off the street. He was talking to himself and crying, but he was saying, "ho, ho, ho" as he cried, so it sounded like laughing at first. He wasn't leaning against anything, just standing in the middle of the porch. I felt very disturbed to see him out there by himself.

Andy's arms suddenly circled my waist. "It's a long way from Arkansas," he said. He kissed the top of my head. The air had cooled off, and there was a slight breeze. It was so humid I wondered whether the smell of jasmine in the air might cling to me, like cologne. Crickets and air conditioners whirred into the night. Through an empty lot and across two streets, you could see the darkened sign of a Thrifty's drugstore.

Andy spoke first. "The best time of day is around eight or nine in the morning, when you can still smell the jasmine." He was gazing toward the street, toward the empty lot. I don't know what he saw.

"You can smell the jasmine now," I said.

"I like night, too," he said, gently. I pulled him down to kiss his cheek. He didn't really acknowledge I'd kissed him; he just moved his eyes shyly down and up again. Every so often since I'd met him, he would become suddenly and momentarily shy, and I think it was a shyness he never showed to others. He nodded his head, and I looked out. Henry was standing on the sidewalk, peering into our window. We stepped out of sight.

The next day, we went out to eat. I dropped by Andy's house after supper, and on the way downstairs we heard Roger asking someone where Andy lived.

"Uh-oh," said Andy. "I heard he's mad at me." He looked frightened, but I felt sort of excited.

"I'll stall him," I said. "I'll seduce him." I ran off before Andy could stop me.

Roger was a chubby man who spoke emphatically, placing

an exclamation point after every sentence. "Where's Andy!"
he said. He seemed to know I was Andy's girlfriend.

"He's not home. I stopped by to see him, but no one's
there." He started by me on the stairs, and I tried to block
him but instead accidentally tripped and fell on my nose.
When I sat up he was looking down on me, seemingly un-
decided whether to help or to go search for Andy.

"It's okay," I said. But my nose really hurt. He knelt and
reached for me. "Watch out," I said. "It feels like it might
fall off."

"I'm good at this!" He pointed to his nose. "I used to be
a boxer! I'm an expert on noses!" He felt my face, said I
was fine, then climbed upstairs as I went down the street to
Andy's car. He wasn't there, but I found him sitting in my
car—he'd broken in.

He said he'd tried one of Roger's frauds for himself, and
Roger found out. It was better if I didn't know specifics, he
said, then shrugged it off, and we went out to eat.

I knew things were bad for him, though. In the next few
weeks he began to get listless and moody. I'd met some of
his friends but didn't know which of them he could count on.
I felt bothered by his work in a way I hadn't before. I cared
that he was making his living at other people's expense, but
not that he was breaking the law. I also cared that he was
profiting from a sort of wasteful violence. That's what I
thought would hurt him eventually, not Roger, not the law.
But I didn't know what to do about it.

When customers came into the lamp shop, I tried to sell
them the lamp that matched them best. The lamps were just
like people: some fat, some svelte, some with funny hats,
and some ostentatiously gilded in gold. Sometimes my boss
plugged in as many lamps as possible, then turned them all
on and sat on a chair with a dreamy, satisfied look on her
face. A good lamp, she said, ought to be subtle and flashy
at the same time. She said she kept at least five lamps in each
room of her home, except the bathrooms and kitchen.

For Andy's birthday, I bought a small handmade ceramic

lamp. We went to a movie in Hollywood. We had to park a few blocks from Hollywood Boulevard. It was a beautiful, clear evening. When we got out of the car, a group of religious chanters was just coming up the sidewalk behind us, and every time we turned a corner, they did, too. Andy laughed, in a rare good mood, but I got paranoid and thought they were chasing us to make us join up. I made Andy run around the block with me to get away. It was hard for him to run because he was laughing so hard. We stopped on Hollywood Boulevard and leaned against a building to catch our breath. But even after we'd rested we continued leaning, feeling suddenly and strangely peaceful. We stayed so long we saw the same cars, full of kids, cruising over and over up and down the street. Every once in a while Andy would say something like "Fifty-seven Chevy—nice car." But mostly we just watched. The lights from the theaters and shops looked garish in the night. A man walked by on his hands. Another man offered us a toaster for five dollars. Andy gave him fifty cents, and the man walked on and offered someone else the toaster for four fifty. Watching the street, I felt very hopeful, not about anything in particular. It was a feeling cut off from all logic and reality.

We didn't go to a movie after all. We walked around, eating pizza, talking. Afterward, we stopped briefly and discussed where to put his lamp. Then he had to go to work, so I went home.

I'd also bought the lamp I'd been wanting. I could afford it because my boss gave me a discount, and also let me buy both lamps on credit. At home, I put my purchase on the staircase but didn't like the effect. I tried everything, but the lamp didn't look good anywhere. I unbraided my hair for bed and got under the sheets. I felt less hopeful now. Police helicopters whirred in the distance, as they did almost every night, and wind feathers brushed over my face from the screen behind. I had that sinking feeling you get when you've spent too much money, or lost something you'll get in trouble for losing, or even said something you can't take back. It seemed like a small victory to have finally been able to buy the lamp.

That night, Roger beat Andy up. Andy came over very late. He knocked quietly; I knew it was him. When I opened the door, the hall light at his back made his swollen face look misshapen. I thought for a second I'd better call the police, but I saw how ridiculous that was. I felt very confused and lost, because not being able to call the police made me feel all rules had been rendered arbitrary and irrelevant.

Andy shut the door and wandered over to the front window to look down on the still street. "Is somebody coming?" I said.

He shook his head no, but kept looking. Just looking, for nothing in particular. He ran his fingertips lightly over his bruised face, almost the way he did when checking to see how well he'd shaved. It was the first time in my life I'd ever seen anyone close to me hurt this way. Once, Ben split his heel, but by accident. There seemed to me to be a different— equally awful, but different—feeling that went with seeing someone hurt intentionally, like the difference between bad luck and evil.

"It was Roger," said Andy. "I asked for it."

"You did not. He's a psycho," I said. We didn't speak. I could hear a noise I heard sometimes at early morning, or late at night, when my own nearby world was sleeping, that noise like millions of leaves vibrating, or like horses running, far away. It was a beautiful noise usually, but tonight I thought it was just cars, or a million people fighting, or something awful. It seemed absurd and petty that Roger had bothered with Andy: Andy couldn't have meant much to Roger's enterprises. I felt sick with hate of Roger, and of all the owners of cars who hired Andy. I know, he made his own choices; but so did they. I reached out and brushed my hand over his face; the bumps felt so odd, tumors under his skin. The street was barren. Somewhere dogs were barking, and an ambulance sounded. I felt really scared, not exactly of what had happened but of the scope of the world, the violence. I went to sit on my staircase while Andy leaned against the window ledge. I just wanted to be close to him. He was tapping something. It reminded me of my grandmother's arthritic clicking knee. The next day Andy told me that I'd fallen asleep and shouted, "Stop hitting me, you witch!" in my sleep.

The next night after work, Andy came over and said everything was okay now: Roger apologized for what he'd done and offered him a good job. Andy decided to go to work full time for Roger. I thought he was crazy, but he was excited— no more crashing cars on hilltops.

Later we went to a party at Roger's house. The house was huge and sat on a hill. Inside, the halls were lined with original art, including three Picasso drawings. There were some very fine paintings, along with some bad paintings by well-known artists. A huge table was covered with ornate silver and crystal bowls filled with Fritos, saltines, and Planter's nuts. While searching for a bathroom, I came upon a room with nothing but mirrors on one wall, and next door there was videotape equipment. When I pushed open the door, someone inside rushed toward me, and I hurried backward "Bathroom," I said, half stumbling, and he pointed me down the hall.

When I returned to the living room, I stood looking out the glass doors to the terrace while Roger, Roger's wife, Andy, and some friends of Roger's talked behind me. It was early December, but there was a heat wave and a strong warm wind. A short way down the hills, white Christmas lights were wound around each tree in a line of palms, making it seem in the night that the trees themselves had disappeared and left fossils of light. I thought, that's what I want to leave when I die. The light-trees leaned in the wind; you could hear the fronds hitting.

I couldn't understand how it was possible Andy and Roger were talking, friends now. Maybe it was because what disturbed Andy most about getting beat up wasn't the physical hurt but the humiliation, and Roger had made up for that. I watched everyone's reflection in the clean glass. Roger was broad, in a dark suit. His wife was lean and perfect, with lots of hair and a long, long neck. Roger scratched his chin. "Mosquitoes in December!" he said, and everyone laughed. Looking at the landscape again, I felt amazed at how all those varied worlds out there coexisted, including the world I lived in, and the world that in the future would touch me only randomly but that Andy, if he accepted Roger as a friend, would accept as his.

"Nice view," said Andy, coming up beside me.

"Let's go home," I said. "Let's leave this place." The room was silent then behind me.

I turned to look at Andy. He appeared hopeful, as if the thought that he could leave hadn't occurred to him, but then his face hardened the way it did when he was working. I turned back around. "Okay, we'll leave in a second," he finally said, but he murmured it as if he were dreaming, and Roger was laughing again behind me.

16

※ When Andy decided to quit Roger a few weeks later, he was scared to stay in his apartment, so we moved to a place closer to downtown Los Angeles. In a strange way, my new building, like my old, was steeped in music. The man next door practiced throwing knives into the wall while listening to Wagner. He was a former child movie star. Sometimes, if the hour was too early or too late, he didn't listen to music as he practiced. I would wake at 6 A.M. and hear the thump, thump, thump of his knives against the wall. Once, I was at his apartment for coffee when the doorbell rang. He jerked his head and gave me a fearful warning face, then sat quietly with his hands palm down on the table until he heard the visitor leave.

In the apartment below lived a girl who couldn't have been more than sixteen or seventeen years old. The girl played opera constantly. She didn't always close the curtains, and if you were outside you could see into her place. She would be sitting in front of her tape player and turntable, changing songs. She'd play a song from an album and switch to a tape just as the first song was ending. On weekends she played disk jockey like that for hours, from when she woke up to when she went to bed.

There were a lot of Chinese immigrants where we lived, and the children all played outside until bedtime. Our first year there, a mass murderer was loose in Los Angeles, and the children stopped playing outside for a while. The murderer had strangled someone across the street, and his presence hung like fine dust over the rows of stucco apartments and rooming houses in the neighborhood. The children made sure to walk home in groups from Chinese school, which many of them attended daily after regular school. In my own building, everyone argued about whether leaving the porch light on at night would attract the murderer's attention or scare him away. I even noticed some of the parents looking at Andy suspiciously when he talked to their children. By and large, though, most people ignored the murderer's existence. He was like a heat wave; you lived with it. When they caught him, the children were back out playing the next day. It was as if the murderer never existed. I loved the children for their adaptability.

Meanwhile Andy started a messenger service which did pretty well. Previously he'd tried other businesses. He kept a number of different kinds of stationery in his desk, with different names on each kind. "Andrew Hamilton Chin, Inc." for the mail-in cold cream business. "Andy Chin" for the mail-in Chinese food recipe enterprise. He took out an ad in the back of a magazine and got seventeen responses. The messenger service was his first success. But I loved him for his failures, too. I loved how he always had a deal cooking, how he *spent* his life like currency to get what he wanted.

My first out-of-town visitor wasn't my parents—they came later—but my brother Walker. Earlier in the year he and some friends from school drew up a suicide pact. When my parents found out, they didn't know whether "this is just a teenage thing or what," but they sent him to Los Angeles a few months later, for a change.

Andy and I decided to take Walker on a vacation to Oregon. Though Highway 99 was less scenic than the ride up the coast, I'd driven on it many times as a child, so we took it up. Some of my parents' friends used to live on the east side of 99, but when the war started, there was a law that Japanese had to move west of the highway, so they packed up all their things and moved across the street. The next year they were interned.

When we reached Oregon, the countryside was all brown cliffs and gray fogs, and I was disappointed. But in a couple of hours we found ourselves between falls of rhododendrons, and you could smell fireplace wood in the cool summer air. The beaches in mid-Oregon were clean, and cooler and more relaxed than the beaches in California. We checked into a place called the Oceanfront Ridge. The ocean was visible from our rooms. We were splurging for Walker.

The afternoon turned overcast, so though it was Sunday the beach remained relatively empty. I called an old friend of mine, Susie, and she met us at the beach with some of her friends—some men in the coast guard and a few women. Most of the women seemed to like the same man. I wished one of them would like Walker, even though he was young.

Susie's boyfriend was named Leo. Susie was giggly and spoke in giggly, squeaky outbursts. She was several years older than Walker, but I could tell he liked her. The next afternoon, while Andy was resting and Leo working, Walker, Susie, and I drove to the house of her sister, who was going to have lunch with us.

When we got to her place, Ellen, the sister, was arguing with her husband. We heard them as we walked toward the door. When Susie knocked, Ellen came to the door, smiled, and said, "Hi, guys. Can you hold on a sec?" She talked in the same squeaky voice as Susie. I didn't think their voices had changed much since we were in grammar school. The only thing about Ellen I remembered besides her voice was that she'd been double-jointed and used to do contortionist tricks for us sometimes if we begged.

Ellen closed the door, and we waited outside. The argument was well under way. In fact, it seemed to be ending, or perhaps it was ending only because of our arrival. In any case, I have no idea what it was about.

We could hear easily from where we stood—Susie hadn't moved after Ellen closed the door.

"I misunderstood," Ellen was saying, with the forced calmness of someone arguing in public.

"How could you have misunderstood?" said her husband, with the same calmness.

Ellen made no sound. I became conscious of the crunching my feet made in the gravel, so I tried to stay very still.

After a long silence, the husband said, "You're a pig, you know. You're insane." He spit out the words, and I thought they'd hurt her as much as a physical strike.

In a moment, I did hear a slap, though who slapped whom I don't know. A little girl stuck out her head after a while. "Susie, Mom says she's not coming after all. Sorry." Inside I could see Ellen's husband, a smaller man than I'd imagined, and not at all nasty-looking.

"Okay, kiddo. See you," said Susie.

We got in the car and left.

"Do they fight like that often, if you don't mind my asking?" Walker said.

"Quite a bit," she said. Then, as if in explanation, she added, "They've been married ten years."

"Doesn't it drive you crazy?"

Susie shrugged. "Of course, I tend to side with her," she said. Again she added, "But they've been married ten years."

"Are they happy?" I asked.

"I wouldn't say that."

"Does he hit her?"

"I wouldn't say that, either," Susie said. She turned to the window at a stop sign, ending the conversation, whose subject was after all none of our business.

The three of us lay on the beach all afternoon. Andy had said he felt like being alone. The beach was full of tourists, but they were quiet tourists. Even when people called each other, they did so in museum tones. A boat, apparently stuck on a sandbar, sat near shore. Several times during the afternoon someone swam out to explore. On the beach, a couple of people set up umbrellas, bright spots of red and yellow against the muted greens and sand tones of the beach and sky.

Susie and Walker took a walk at sunset, so I swam out to the boat. I could smell it as I neared, a moldy, old, sad smell. On deck, the floor was damp and blackened, the steering wheel corroded. A plastic flag whipped in the wind. For a moment I stared at the flag, the only moving thing except for myself on board. I gasped when I saw a pair of children's shoes hanging from a nail—I'd thought they were feet hanging down. Inside the shoes I found a damp pair of socks wrapped around two quarters, a nickel, a penny. The boat jolted with each wave. The shoes had an eeriness about them, and it didn't surprise me that none of the afternoon's explorers had taken the money. I got the feeling the shoes' owner had passed away; and out of respect for him or her, I re-wrapped the coins and replaced them. There was something about the care with which the socks were wrapped that indicated a conscientious, serious child; also, something about the fifty-six cents touched me, for at one time I believed that pennies could buy a great deal indeed and so deserved to be wrapped carefully.

I sat down and leaned against the side of the boat, hugging my knees. I wished the boat would float out and I could be even more alone. But then I got up, jumped into the water, and swam to shore. A wave hit me hard, and I fell. Angry, I waited for the next big wave, and when it hit I hit back. A couple of men sat on a flat rock up the beach, and I hesitated before leaving the water. At first I thought the men were Andy and Walker, then I didn't think so, then I did. Beach lights illuminated the sand, but I didn't have on my glasses.

They didn't watch me walk toward them, but when I sat down, Andy unfolded a blanket to wrap around me.

"What'd you do all day?" I said.

"Lying around in the sun."

He looked sleepy, dreamy, relaxed, and rubbed my dripping hair with the blanket. Walker stretched and lay down on a blanket in the sand.

"Where's Susie?"

"Eating with Leo and them. Wanna go?" said Andy.

"I'm not hungry."

A wind blew. I pulled the blanket closer.

"Anything special on board?" said Walker.

"Nothing much. Have you been out there?"

He shook his head. "Susie was out there earlier. I saw her from my window. I got the feeling she wanted to be alone."

"How long have you guys been sitting out here?"

Andy glanced at his watch, squinted at the ocean. "A while," he said. He was in a sweet mood and a bad one at the same time. I got the feeling Walker was becoming a burden. I knew they'd had words the day before.

I told him about the argument earlier between Ellen and her husband. "I can see how Susie would be used to the whole thing by now, but I keep thinking if it were my sister, I'd be upset. It bothered me how unconcerned Susie was."

Andy nodded. Walker turned over on his stomach. He was watching as Susie and Leo approached from down the beach. "It's *hard*," he said. "I figure she can be whatever the fuck she wants."

I'd never heard Walker swear before. It sounded funny. He watched furtively as Susie and Leo came down the sand. Two thoughts occurred to me. I replayed Susie's words about her sister's marriage, replayed the cadence and intonation, and realized she meant not that it was natural for a couple married ten years to fight the way Ellen and her husband did, but that for ten years Susie tried to change her sister's life, and now she realized she never would. The second thing that occurred to me, for no reason, was how in the boat I couldn't have floated out if I'd wanted to, since Andy and Walker were watching, protecting.

My bad eyes softly obscured the sand and water. I could barely make out the points of light on the horizon. Under the beach lights, huge moths flew back and forth. They looked like giant fireflies, because every time they flew under the lamps they appeared to light up. Walker jumped up and ran toward the water. "I'm swimming to the boat!" he shouted. I got a little thrill, partly because I was worried about him swimming in the dark, partly because he'd shouted happily and his happiness thrilled me.

When Walker was little, he was never more happy than when he was alone. Sometimes I came upon him by himself, enraptured by some little project. Just as frequently I came upon him while he was talking to himself, in a fantasy. Walker was always the one you could trust: he never broke a promise or told on you, and if someone broke a promise to him, he wouldn't speak to that person, sometimes all week. He climbed into the boat and sat down. I could no longer see him.

By the time he got back, we were all getting drunk. He didn't drink, just lay on the blanket. I studied his slender back against the blanket. I couldn't stop staring at him. Finally he "tagged" me, turned around right when I was staring. "I'm okay," he said.

When I drink and get weepy-eyed at the same time, my eyes swell up. I felt a drunken self-pity, sorry for *myself* because I thought Walker was suicidal. I wanted someone to fuss over me and make me feel better. Susie looked at me, fascinated, and said, "Your eyes are so swollen. You look like a salamander or something."

We were terribly drunk. Everyone leaned in a little bit. Even Walker, from his blanket, eyed me curiously. Leo leaned in until our noses almost touched. "She does! She does look like a salamander!"

Susie said, "Her left eye is less swollen. Her left eye looks like a salamander's, and her right eye looks like a toad's."

That seemed to be the final word on the subject, and everyone returned to drinking. Walker smiled at me, and I couldn't help smiling back.

Andy started shaking his head and laughing, and then we were all laughing. Susie switched on a radio, and during one song she squealed, "This song reminds me of carrots."

"I'm not going to ask why," said Leo, but in a few minutes he said, "I can't stand it. Tell me, why did that song remind you of carrots?"

She said, as if the answer were obvious, "Because when

it was popular I had a vitamin A deficiency and I had to eat tons of carrots.''

We drank more, and on the next song Leo raised his bottle and shouted, ''I'm reminded of asparagus!'' Susie got Walker so drunk we had to carry him back to his hotel room.

We'd entered Oregon in the morning, and left a few afternoons later, driving through a landscape filled with layers of greens reflecting off the waters. I read once that there were three main rivers in the country, one on the West Coast, one on the East, and one in the Midwest. The rivers, made up of migrant farmworkers, traveled down the country every year during the growing season. My brother, Andy, and I drove home through the Western river. Some of the fields were being harvested; in others, sprigs of green shot up from black soil, the green and black stretching into the horizon until the colors became part of the circle of vanishing points around the car. ''It's just the same as it used to be,'' said Walker, but I knew he was wrong.

17

✳✳ "It looks like it always does," said Walker. The green sprigs looked bright against the black soil.

"Are you sure this is the right road?" said my mother.

"Get off this road—get off it now," said Obāsan. "Get. Off. This. Road." She batted my ears for emphasis. She was having one of her bad feelings about this street. My mother and father looked at each other. Peter shot up, suddenly awake. He looked terrified.

"Peter doesn't like this place, either," I said.

"I can't even find it on the map," said my mother.

Charlie-O made a sharp turn and drove back toward the highway. This road *was* spooky, stunning but totally empty, no people anywhere. My father was doing ninety by the time he finally caught the highway again. All this was neither too unusual nor, I think, unreasonable. I really believe some motels, some restaurants and roads, would have brought us bad luck if we used them.

We were on our way that morning to look at model homes. As a lark, we decided to go see the homes after reading a billboard advertisement. We found the place a couple of hours before lunch and parked in front.

A woman with lipstick on her top teeth came to greet us and show the four houses. "What are you looking for?" was her first question. Then: "And what do you do?" "What a nice family. Are you expecting more?" "How much are you hoping to spend?'' My parents smiled shyly. ''We're just looking, actually.'' ''Different things.'' ''Yes, I'd like more,'' said my father. ''No,'' said my mother. And: ''We're not sure.''

All of us except the woman and Obāsan took off our shoes as we entered the houses. Each house was more beguiling than the one before. The last one had splendid white carpets, and chairs I thought were so old they were made before Obāsan was born. Ben had to explain they were only copies. The nicest thing about the house was how from the bedroom windows upstairs you could see some faraway trees with white bark that looked blue in the morning. ''Look!'' I said to my parents. ''Blue trees.'' They smiled shakily. My parents were nervous. The woman was getting impatient. ''*What* are you looking for?'' ''*How* much are you expecting to spend?'' Of course, she could see by now we couldn't really afford a house.

We got in the car again, feeling a little awed, a little hopeful and humiliated. We were hopeful because the beautiful houses made us feel that way.

My grandmother wrote in her diary, her hand shaking whenever we went over a bump. She didn't write much: ''We looked at model homes today. Mariko is sad. Did I do the wrong thing forcing her into marriage? No, I don't think so. Anyway, it's too late now.'' I read that when I was grown up.

That was a typical entry from those days. Her entries before then were vigorous and certain, full of answers and proclamations. Later, around the time we saw the houses, her entries were filled with both questions and answers, and finally, toward the end of her life, only questions. I thought you grew more certain with age, but she grew less.

The wind was blowing hard—birds, clouds, cars, all going in the same direction. A sudden gust of wind made a dandelion field explode.

Ben leaned out the window and started crowing, and Walker started to whinny. I barked at the top of my lungs. Every so often we'd look at our parents and grandmother, waiting for someone to quiet us, or, in the case of Obāsan, to pummel us. For once, she didn't. She had her hand out the window, trying to catch dandelion seeds.

In the evening we watched the farmworkers leaving the fields. Walker stared out the window, in a trance, listening for something. He could stare at anything, even a single hair lying on a table, but mostly he preferred to stare at people. Though Obāsan was napping, she shook and thrashed in her sleep, and bonked me twice on the nose by accident. I pushed her away and stuck my head out the window. At the beginning and end of the day, there was always something terribly serious about the farmworkers, even more so than when they were working. They reminded me of animals migrating across a field; in transit. They were moving from the hard life just past to the life, maybe harder, to come.

18

※ I talked to a ghost once, but he didn't talk back. I asked the ghost questions, and then I told him I hated him. The ghost was my real father, who'd died a month earlier. We sat on a curb and ate candy bars together. I ate the real thing; he ate candy you couldn't see through exactly but that wavered whenever the wind blew. By the time we parted, I no longer hated him. Or I realized it wasn't as simple as that. He was standing next to his rose-colored convertible; he'd always liked racy cars. The top was down. It was a lovely night—hazy, but the sort of haze that makes the air itself seem to be all different colors.

This happened in Arizona when I was twenty-one—the year before I finally decided to go to college. My father, whom I called Jack, died in Barstow, California. That's also where he was living, with his wife and kids, when he first met my mother the year before my birth.

When Jack was alive, he was "in vending machines," as my mother used to say, when she said anything about him at all. He owned and serviced a vending-machine route, and when he died, his wife, whom I hardly knew, asked me to take over the route until she could sell it. A vending-machine route had to be kept alive, she said. If the machines stayed empty too long, the customers—gas stations, bus stops, offices, and schools—might let new vendors move in. Even if that didn't happen, the route would shrivel and die without constant servicing. Jack and his wife had two sons, but neither of them could get away just then, and his wife was in bad health. For helping her, she promised me a very small percentage of the profits from the sale of the business. The route was in California, Arizona, and Nevada, and it was while I was servicing it that I saw the ghost. The last time I'd seen Jack alive, I was in high school and visiting my mother's relatives in Los Angeles. Even after I moved to California, I spoke to him only a couple of times. Charlie-O was the one who was "Dad."

Jack's wife sent all his business papers, maps, keys, and files to me, and I tried to figure everything out. Jack used codes I couldn't always understand for the machine's keys. I planned to organize for a couple of days before I left to service the route; it ended up taking me a week. As I sat at my desk and started decoding, I felt surreptitious and secretive, like a spy, but that illusion was destroyed by the din of the opera from below and the knives thumping on the other side of the wall. Andy and I kept discussing moving, but we never got around to it.

I wrote my mother about all this, and she called me one night while I was decoding. "Honey, your dad says he would be glad to go with you on the route," she said.

I heard his voice in the background, saying, "Tell her things aren't that busy at work for me right now." But I knew his garage was thriving and he never had any time.

"I can do it myself," I said. Actually, I had some doubts about that, but I didn't want to admit them to my parents.

I heard Charlie-O, closer to the phone now, saying, "What did she say?"

My mother said, "Well, your dad just thought maybe you wouldn't want to be alone."

I asked whether he would come just until I felt comfortable, and he agreed. I didn't doubt he wanted to help me, but I also thought he was curious about the man he had perceived as a rival: when he married my mother, she still loved Jack. Though she once told me she loved my father, I wasn't really sure. A few months earlier, when my parents had visited Andy and me, she kept staring at us in a funny way. Later, when I asked what made her stare, she said we'd both had the same look on our faces, as if we'd been washed over with the same water. I used to try to picture her with Jack, both of them washed over with the same water.

My dad and I left Los Angeles on one of those hot, ashy days when the surrounding hills are burning with brushfires and a feeling of siege has settled on the whole city. The fires filled me with languor and restlessness, so it was a good time to leave.

Since the time I moved out of my aunt's, I had seen little of my family; it took me by surprise how naturally and quickly new people covered the surface of my life. My dad and I didn't talk much on the phone, and though my mother and I wrote, Charlie-O and I never did anymore. We had at first, but according to Ben, whenever my dad received a letter from me he got a weary look on his face, the way he did when he had to do a chore like filling out tax forms. He always wrote me back, but I knew it was a burden. "It's almost as bad as having to read a book," my brother told me he'd said.

I had worked out a logical route, to cover the territory in the most efficient way. The first day, our stops were mainly gas stations, plus a couple of offices. Mostly small stuff. Our last stop, in the evening, was a Chinese-Italian restaurant. The restaurant had live entertainment—a man in a bow tie singing ballads. Signs hanging inside and out said if you bought two entrées you got the second free.

"Let's eat here," said Charlie-O. "A free meal." Bargains always delighted him in ways that were embarrassing or that seemed to me out of proportion to the money saved. Once when I was younger, a friend of his offered him some spare car parts for his business, on condition he pick them up right away. Our own car was being fixed at the time, so he brought my brothers and me to his friend's house to help carry the parts. On our way back, we walked through town, one of my brothers carrying a carburetor, another brother, my father, and I carrying a blue car door, and Peter carrying a hubcap he kept trying to balance on his head.

"It's not really a free meal," I said. He mumbled something I couldn't quite make out, but it sounded like "Killjoy." "Oh, all right," I said.

My dad ordered sweet-and-sour pork with spaghetti for twelve ninety-five, and I wanted to order a vegetable plate.

"That's only five ninety-five," said my dad. "Besides, didn't you tell me when you were in high school that eating too many vegetables would make your complexion orange?"

"It's what I feel like eating."

"You had a date with Tan, or Spam, or whatever you used to call him, and you wouldn't eat any carrots all week."

"Tan," I said, but he was looking at the menu.

The waitress came, and I asked for the vegetable plate. Charlie-O looked crestfallen. "Don't you feel like shrimp? Look, here's some great shrimp for fourteen ninety-five." His face, always changeable, looked hopeful now. I gave in, which didn't seem to surprise him.

The shrimp, supposed to be marinated in ginger sauce, arrived bathed in ketchup, but my dad didn't want me to return it. "We got a free meal!" he said.

When we finished eating, we went into the foyer, where I had to climb onto the cigarette machine to reach the lock on the candy machine. Jack must have done the same thing dozens of times. "Can you hand me a screwdriver?" I said. "The lock is stuck." My dad didn't answer, and when I looked down, he was staring glassy-eyed out a window into the parking lot.

"You know, sometimes I have thoughts so big they scare me," he said.

A couple of customers walked by and gave each other a look on the way out. "The screwdriver?" I said. Charlie-O stopped staring. "What was the big thought?"

"I don't know. I can't explain it. It's gone now, anyway."

"About Mom?"

"Maybe."

He handed me the screwdriver. "So have you thought any

more about going back to school?'' he said. He spoke tentatively, perhaps afraid I would lose my temper and say as I always did that it was *my* life. ''No'' was all I said.

His face took on a sad aspect, and I wondered whether he was having a different kind of thought now—a practical, unhappy one. He never finished high school himself, and I think he felt going to college would guarantee me my place in the world. Maybe he worried I might end up unhappy, the way he thought my mother was.

Many of the machines we filled were in small towns, clusters of one-story buildings surrounded by yellowed weeds. The buildings had cracked stucco walls of pink, yellow, or white, and nearly all the windows in all the buildings were open, the curtains behind them shivering in the breeze. The children I saw always appeared to me tan and curious without being either healthy or alert, and the houses, as if they were organic, blended into the fields. In the background there were water towers, silver globes protecting the towns from the surrounding desert. At night the scenery was bare but not barren. There were no lights along the highway, and sometimes it was hard to tell we were in a real car, because the scenery on either side changed hardly at all. It was like one of those pretend cars in arcades, where you have a seat and a steering wheel. When trucks passed us, their emblems hung surreally in the blackness between the headlights.

One day in the car, my dad said he'd already stayed away from the garage longer than he'd planned to. But he quickly added that he would be glad to continue the route with me. Who knows what he really wanted to do? I told him I thought I could handle things by myself now. There was a machine in an Arizona bus-stop restaurant we'd reach in a few more hours, and my dad decided to catch a bus back to Arkansas from there. When we got to the restaurant's address, I asked a passerby where the place was, and he pointed to a white frame house and said, ''Second floor.'' I hesitated, because there was no sign anywhere, and he said again, this time irritably, "Second floor." We followed his directions and found a small, quiet, dark restaurant up a flight of squeaky stairs. A young girl served us. She lingered at our table, eager to talk. She wanted to know where we were from and what we did. Ordinarily my dad was the talkative one, but this time I answered. He'd been looking more tired each day.

"So you're only halfway done with the route," he said, after the girl left. "Think you can hold out?"

"I'm fine. I kind of like it."

He was quiet again. A little boy at the next table dropped a container of milk and knocked over his chair as he caught the milk, which splattered all over his face. His mother told him to sit still, and he smiled at me, sly and angelic.

When the bus came, we went downstairs. Charlie-O idly leaned over and knocked on one of the wheels of the bus. He examined the tread, nodded and grunted approvingly, then got that glassy-eyed look again.

"What are you thinking about?" I said.

"To tell you the truth, I was thinking did you know your mother had an affair once?"

I hesitated, then said, "I know."

"Did you know I almost had one, too, a couple of years ago?"

I shook my head, though his back was to me now. I felt sick and sad inside to hear this, and I was glad he didn't turn to look at me.

He shrugged. "It doesn't matter. We went out to dinner a couple of times. See, I wanted to tell you because nothing happened. See, your mother told me once how she ended with Jack. She said he took her to his house one day, and on the wall was this thing called a Wish List. It had writing all over it, like 'toy truck' and 'stuffed animal,' and Jack's wife had written 'a new couch for my birthday.' Your mother was about seventeen years old. A few weeks later, he took her there again, and a new couch was sitting in the living room. His wife wanted this thing for the house, and he got it for her, and that made your mother see for the first time the way his wife was connected to him and the way he was connected to her. She and Jack went into the bedroom then, but the whole time she just lay there feeling sad. So I kept thinking about that when I met this other lady, and somehow that stuff your mother told me meant more to me than the other things, the things she did to me.'' He turned to me and became energized for the first time in days. "It's wrong!" he said. "Two people get married! They get married. Period.''

There had always been something primitive about his morality; it was as if his need for a moral order were as strong as the need for food and water. When I was growing up, I always felt sheltered by his convictions, and by his belief that all his children would grow up "good." Whenever we did something "bad" or "wrong," he wasn't so much disappointed as confused and disbelieving. I guess most people never learn the best or worst they're capable of. What I learned from letting Obāsan die so long ago was something about the possibilities for "bad" in me. That changed me somehow.

"Nuh my kihs r hap," he mumbled.

"I'm sorry?"

"Nothing.''

"I hate it when people won't tell me what they just said.''

"I said not all my kids are happy.'' He looked at me hopefully.

"We're all happy,'' I said, and he smiled a tiny satisfied smile.

As he was about to get on the bus, he reached into his wallet and took out all the money in there: twelve dollars. "Here, you might need some cash.''

"Dad, I'm grown up, I work, I have money—remember?" I said. "Plus, I've got all the change from the machines.''

"Don't worry, I have credit cards,'' he said, handing me the bills. As he was going up the bus steps, he paused and turned and said plaintively, "Now, don't you write me.'' Then he took his seat.

After the bus left, I walked back upstairs to the restaurant. I felt greasy and ragged, and I noticed spots on my blouse and bruises on my hands from working. A long time ago, a friend of mine had lived on the floor above a cafeteria that also served as a bus station. Often the girl used to wash up before bed in the public bathroom below her home. We used to help her parents around the cafeteria. When I stayed over-night with her, we spied on the passengers, laughing at how tired they looked and at all the different ways people can look tired. They sat there yawning and disheveled, eating chili or mashed potatoes at 4 A.M. I studied the people carefully. That's who I want to be, I would think, or, There's a family I wish were mine, or, Wherever that family is going is where I want to go.

The girl from the restaurant talked with me while I filled the candy machines. She said her town was bigger than it looked, maybe ten thousand people. She said she was fifteen, then seemed to be studying my face to see whether I believed her. Before I left, I gave her a bottle of clear nail polish and she gave me a few breakfast rolls she sneaked out of the kitchen.

Work grew less complex as time passed, because the more machines I serviced, the fewer keys remained that I hadn't matched with a machine. I worked harder, but I also felt relaxed. I would sit on the car in the sun eating candy bars and figuring things out—working on adjustments to my route, figuring out how much money I'd spent. Jack's wife was going to reimburse me for my expenses. Using Jack's note-books, I saw his handwriting change over time, the slant moving from right to left. Occasionally there was a note in the margins: "Need new lock for C-24. . . . New man try-ing to take over territory A-5." I wondered what *he* had written on the Wish List.

I knew I didn't have to service all the machines. Origi-nally, I'd planned to leave some, doing only enough to keep the route salable. But then I decided to do them all anyway, just for the obsession of it. A couple of the most out-of-the-way places were tiny offices for which Jack had simply laid out candy on shelves, with no machines, and the office work-ers paid on the honor system. He'd gotten to know the people in those offices better than the people at his more profitable locations. I thought maybe he'd told some of those smaller customers about me, maybe showed them pictures, if he carried any. In any case, "Jack's girl" is what a couple of them called me.

I saw my father's ghost when I was almost finished with the route, at one of those out-of-the-way places I'd considered not servicing. Earlier that night, someone kept tailgating me, though the road was empty and he easily could have passed. I slowed, he slowed, I pulled over, and he stopped rather than pass. Finally I turned onto a side road and he sped on.

It was very late, but I had only two more stops for the night. The next-to-the-last one was a gas station; it had two machines, one with snacks like potato chips and cookies, and one with candy bars and gum. I was testing keys when I suddenly noticed Jack standing next to me, at a third vending machine, which appeared out of nowhere. I think I screamed and ran a few steps toward my car, but something made me stop and turn. Jack was shaking his keys, but I heard no jingling. "Jack?" I called. I walked back. His image was not quite right. I realized he was a ghost when the wind came up but didn't muss his hair, just made his whole body flow to the side and back. His personality seemed to flow back and forth, as well: at first, with his cagey glances to one side, he reminded me of a weasel; then he smiled to himself and seemed almost innocent. I looked around and behind me and saw nothing, no one. I'd never met a ghost before, but I figured the thing to do was try to communicate. I wasn't scared; after all, it was my father, even if I did hardly know him. "So, have you seen my grandmother around?" I said, but he didn't answer. Maybe he wanted to talk about work. "Do you always come out here to service this machine, even though it's so out of the way?" Like me, he'd probably been tempted to skip it. But I bet he never did. He needed to be diligent for a business like this to work, I realized. I'd never thought about that before. The first time I remember seeing him, he was driving a convertible, and I guessed he didn't need to worry much about money. It had probably been important for him to appear that way to people.

He began putting coins into the machine and checking each candy slot to make sure nothing was out of order. Before he put his key into the lock, he studied the key, blew on the metal, shined it with his shirt. He paused for a split second, and I realized it was to see whether he could catch a piece of his reflection in the key.

"I see your car over there," I said. "You were following me earlier." My voice sounded the way it always did, but it also sounded strange, because I was basically talking to myself. We worked silently together.

When he was finished, he sat on the gas station curb, and I joined him. Across the road, the ground was so flat it exhilarated me, the way it went on and on. We both tore open a candy-bar wrapper. I had never eaten so much candy in my life. For the last couple of weeks, I'd been living mostly on candy bars and milk.

Jack ate appreciatively, as if chocolate were his favorite food. I reached out and ran my hand through him, only it didn't go through, exactly; it just stretched him out in the middle, as if he were elastic. I asked him about my mother, what she had been like and how much he had loved her, and when he still didn't answer, I told him I hated him for putting a curse on my dad's life. He tore the wrapper on his candy bar lower and wiped his mouth with his shirt. It seemed like such a lonely life suddenly: before he died he used to do exactly what he was doing now that he was dead, again and again for twenty years. He did it so many times he still couldn't break the habit. A moth flitted back and forth through his nose. I brushed it away.

"Well, if you're just going to be sitting there, we ought to talk," I said. "Do you have any questions? Shall I tell you about my brothers? Do you want to hear about my boyfriend?"

He nodded at an appropriate moment, but I guess it was just coincidence. "My boyfriend's name is Andy Chin. He lives with me. He's moody, but I wouldn't say he has a bad temper. Sometimes we talk about having a baby and about what kind of house we'd like. But the thing is, I want to move up north and he wants to stay in Los Angeles.'' Jack sneezed soundlessly. "Bless you,'' I said. "Did I ever show you any pictures of my brothers? Walker's pretty quiet, but he's not really shy, the way he used to be. He just doesn't like to talk to people if they don't interest him. Ben's the opposite. He has too many friends. Walker and Ben are in high school. Peter's in grammar school. He skipped a grade because he's so smart.'' I couldn't help adding, "I bet neither of your sons skipped a grade.''

I took a breath. I noticed for the first time that Jack was quite young, maybe about my age or a few years older. He was younger than I could remember ever having seen him. That meant he'd probably just bought the candy route. I think he met my mother around that time. But perhaps that was still in the future for him, a few months or years away. I hadn't been born yet as he sat there. When my mother fell in love with Jack, she must have realized how young they were and that things wouldn't turn out well. But she didn't care. I liked to think of her then, not caring.

Jack got up and went to his car, brushed it with his hand, admired it. He took out a small notebook and started writing. I wondered where he was going now. The moon, cut in half by a cloud, was two semicircles. Down the highway past the gas station sat a couple of small signs, the back of a billboard, another gas station, and then the highway curved into the night. In the other direction there were no signs and no buildings, just the highway cutting through the fields of yellowed grass. The grass was so pale with dryness it looked almost snow-covered.

Jack started scribbling in a bigger notebook, probably one that I later read. I got angry again, because he wouldn't or couldn't pay attention to me. "If it weren't for you, maybe my mother would have loved my dad more,'' I said. But that didn't quite make sense. I tried to figure why not: I was at Max's Gasamat, but Jack wasn't, although in a way he was, and I wouldn't be there if it weren't for him, since he was, even though he . . . What time was it? I was getting sleepy. The dry air smelled faintly of gasoline. I still had another stop, and for a moment I began to worry about my work and forgot about Jack. I tried to calculate from the night sky what time it was, but then I gave up. It didn't matter; it was high time I left.

About the Author

Cynthia Kadohata was born in Chicago. Her stories have appeared in *The New Yorker*, *Grand Street*, and *The Pennsylvania Review*. She lives in Manhattan.